MYSTERY AT BLUFF COTTAGE

To start afresh after being recently widowed, Penny Lawson leaves the city with her small son and returns to the scene of many happy childhood years. She moves into the now isolated and neglected caretaker's cottage, overlooking the sea, and accepts the help and friendship of persuasive estate agent Lance Patrick. But his actions soon lead her to question his motives. And when an old school friend arrives unexpectedly, her peace is completely shattered . . .

JO JAMES

MYSTERY AT BLUFF COTTAGE

Complete and Unabridged

LINFORD
Leicester

First published in Great Britain in 2000

First Linford Edition
published 2004

British Library CIP Data

James, Jo,
    Mystery at Bluff cottage.—Large print ed.—
Linford romance library
    1. Love stories
    2. Large type books
    I. Title
    823.9'2 [F]

ISBN 1–84395–469–9

Published by
F. A. Thorpe (Publishing)
Anstey, Leicestershire

Set by Words & Graphics Ltd.
Anstey, Leicestershire
Printed and bound in Great Britain by
T. J. International Ltd., Padstow, Cornwall

This book is printed on acid-free paper

1

Penny paused outside the real estate agency. The late Australian winter wind whipped up the dust and blew it against the shopfront. She readjusted her knitted cap as she scanned the posted properties for sale. There was no mention of Bluff Cottage. Disappointed, she re-read the notices, without success.

Earlier today, when she'd visited the Bluff, out in front of the property stood a large, rusting **For Sale** sign. In an instant, she was assailed by an undeniable desire to own it. On the drive back to Sandy Bluff, she was already planning Jamie's introduction to the adventure of living close to the sea, and of spending long, lazy days cleaning up the garden and renovating the house. It felt so right, urgent, almost.

Penny crossed her fingers as she

entered the real estate agency. All was silent inside. When no-one came to attend to her, she cleared her throat quite loudly and then called, 'Hello, is anyone in?'

Still no response. Spotting a bell at the end of the high counter, she gave it a jolly good thump. A man emerged from the rear, tall, with a thatch of dark, unruly hair, deep blue eyes which glittered impatiently from his beachcomber complexion.

'Yes,' he demanded from the doorway, his voice confirming the irritation reflected in his eyes.

His demeanour set Penny back, but only for a few seconds.

'I'm interested in buying one of your properties.'

'And here was I thinking, with the bell ringing so loudly, there must have been a fire.'

She stared at him coldly.

'If that's how you treat your customers . . . ' she began.

'Look, I'm sorry, but I'm in the

middle of a complex computer operation. The salesperson is at lunch. He should be back shortly. Take a seat. Help yourself to the magazines.'

'Can't you help?' she snapped. 'I'm down from Melbourne and I've got a three-hour drive home. I don't have time to wait around.'

'He shouldn't be that long. I have to get back to my project.'

'But you do work here?'

Hoping persuasion might move him, she toned down her voice, swept him a smile.

'Yes,' he said curtly.

Apparently her tactics hadn't succeeded. She flashed him a wider smile.

'Perhaps you can answer a few questions then.'

He heaved broad shoulders.

'Go for it. What's your problem?'

'No problem. I'm interested in buying the cottage out at the Bluff.'

The impatience disappeared, his eyes narrowed. He came out to the counter.

'Bluff Cottage? What's the big attraction about that particular property?'

'You do know it then? You are a salesman?'

'Do you usually question people's word? Sure I'm a salesman, but I'm a bit out of touch because I've been assigned to putting in a computer system. That's how I happen to know that Bluff Cottage isn't for sale.'

A wave of disappointment shot through her.

'But there's a sign outside the property which says it is for sale.'

'It probably hasn't been taken down, that's all. If you hang around, Greg McCann will show you some other desirable properties when he returns. If you'll excuse me, I'm busy. Sorry.'

He swung away, retreating to the back room. Penny felt so cross, she'd have to be careful she didn't start behaving in bad grace.

'I'm sorry, too. What kind of business are you running here? Outdated signs, no salespeople on hand. Whatever

4

happened to service in these parts? Years ago it used to be a very obliging little town.'

He turned back to her.

'So you're familiar with this area? You lived here?'

'I know it well. I used to spend school holidays at the cottage.'

Her enthusiasm led her on.

'My girlfriend boarded in town with us during the school week. I used to come home with her at weekends and holidays. Her father managed the big estate, Brokenridge, and they lived at the cottage, which was part of the property in those days.'

'Well, that is interesting.'

His cynical answer left her stranded for words. She said the first thing which came into her mind.

'You asked me a question. You received an answer. I thought you might be interested in the history of the area.'

She wasn't sure why he laughed.

'I'm more interested in why you've suddenly decided you want to come back here to live. Tell me,' he said and appraised her with steely blue eyes, 'why would you want that particular cottage when you can take your pick of half a dozen other places along the coast at bargain winter prices? It's rundown, out of town and, if you'll pardon me, the southerlies that blow on the Bluff would lift someone small like you right off your feet.'

He wasn't willing to help her, but he obviously knew a lot about the district.

'So you've been up to the cottage,' she replied. 'You sound as if you know the area well. I want the cottage, if you must know, because it has fantastic views, wonderful memories.'

She tilted her chin, slightly embarrassed, but not afraid to be honest.

'I also thought, because it needs work, it might be in my price bracket. In my mind I was already planning to do it up over time.'

She smiled briefly, determined not to let him know how cross she felt with him.

'I came down here on impulse, but when I saw the **For Sale** sign, I got excited.'

Suddenly, it hit her she was giving up too easily, allowing this impatient man to brush her off like a fly. She tried again, smiling, but without much enthusiasm.

'The property is clearly marked for sale, and I'm sure it hasn't been lived in for ages. I'd like to talk to the manager. I expect he'll be more helpful.'

'He's out at lunch. I'm in charge at the moment. The name is Lance Patrick. So what in particular were you planning to take up with the manager?'

Penny swallowed. The business didn't have much of a chance with him as front man. Come to think of it, he didn't look or act like a real estate man. He wore jeans, an open-necked, lightly-checked sports shirt, its sleeves rolled to the elbows, as if to show off his tanned, muscled arms. And on what might otherwise have been a handsome face, there sat an almost permanent look of impatience.

Salesmen were supposed to be super-friendly, keen to do business. This one would never pass the personality test. Lance Patrick couldn't sell water to a drought-stricken town. She amended that. With his unnerving smile, certain women were likely to buy anything from him. And she had a feeling he thought she was one of them.

'If you're in charge, you can give the name of the new owner, please. While I'm down here I might as well visit and see if I can persuade him, or her, to sell.'

'So you're that keen on the old place, are you?' he said.

'Yes.'

He came back to the counter.

'Tell you what. I think I could arrange for you to rent it for a bit. I'll have a word with the owner. He's a friend of mine. He lives inland from here, and only uses it for weekend fishing trips. Another winter at the Bluff might see him out, if you're prepared to wait to purchase.'

The man confused Penny. One minute the place wasn't for sale, the next he was offering to rent it to her, but, his odd behaviour aside, bottom line, she had this strange, compulsive yearning to own the cottage.

'Renting doesn't suit me. I want to do the old place up,' she insisted. 'I'd need a good hot water system, adequate heating. As I remember it, it gets very cold this time of year. The owner won't want to go to that expense for a tenant, and I can't afford to install new facilities, unless I'm sure he'll sell eventually, Mr Patrick.'

'Let me talk to the owner. He may be interested in putting in a few mod cons. It'll add to the value of the place when he's ready to sell. Meantime, Miss . . . I don't think I got your name.'

'It's Mrs . . . er . . . Penelope Lawson,' she said firmly.

She disliked the name Penelope. Her mother had chosen it because the heroines in the novels she read had similar names. As a kid, for fun, her friend, Shelley, had called her Lady Penelope from The Thunderbirds, but as Penny got older, the title no longer amused her. Her friends often used it to let her know when she was taking herself too seriously. It always succeeded in replanting her two feet back on solid ground. She half expected this supercilious individual to make a mocking reference to it now, but his mind seemed to be elsewhere.

'Mrs Lawson, won't your husband want to see the house before you make any decisions?'

Brad was dead, killed in a road accident. She and her son, Jamie, had walked away from the car, traumatised, but physically unharmed — a miracle, the paramedics told her. It convinced Penny that she and Jamie had been given a second chance at life, and she had determined not to waste it.

Don't think about Brad, she lectured herself. You've clawed your way back into the world. You're doing fine.

She found the courage to say, in a whisper, 'No, I'm a widow.'

His features softened. He felt sorry for her. Everyone did, and after six months, she had begun to dread sympathy, for it always brought tears to her eyes. Don't let it happen, not in front of this man, she prayed silently.

'OK, then, why don't I drive you out to the old place? We can look over it together, make sure it's what you want, and if it is, we can list the things which need doing before you move in. Then I can take it up with ... er ... the current owner.'

It sounded unusual. He was acting oddly, suddenly being more helpful. Why? Whatever the answer, she had no intention of going all the way home without exploring every possibility.

Earlier, standing on the cliff front, the collar of her jacket turned up against the southerly, one steadying hand on her car, she'd tasted the salty spray on her lips, felt the wind rush through her hair, and experienced an overwhelming conviction that she was meant to visit the Bluff today, meant to find the cottage for sale, meant to return and settle at Sandy Bluff, and meant to raise her four-year-old son here in the clean, fresh air.

Of course she'd go with Patrick to the cottage, but not in his car. These days she trusted no-one behind the wheel but herself. Apart from that it was lonely out there at the Bluff and she knew almost nothing about him.

'So what do you say about visiting the cottage? Do we or don't we go?' he repeated.

He glanced at his watch, as if the impatience in his blue eyes hadn't already told her she was wasting his precious time.

'You lead the way, Mr Patrick. I'll follow in my car. That way I can get back on the road home without returning to town. Can we leave now, or do you have to wait for your sales manager to get back?'

'I always say there's no time like the present. I'll turn the open sign on the door to closed. That should fix it. My car is parked out back. It's a dark blue Ford. I'll bring it around to the front.'

He went across to the entrance, reversed the open sign and held the door for her.

'Aren't you worried about losing customers?'

Her office training and her curiosity got the better of her. She expected him to tell her to mind her own business. Instead, he smiled down at her. The impatient blue eyes softened.

'You're a real little worrier, aren't you, Mrs Lawson? The business won't go broke while we're away.'

She returned his smile, raised one brow and slipped under his arm which held open the door, and out on to the street. There she could breathe deeply of the cool air, for after he'd smiled at her, she'd felt hot and uncomfortable. But in her anxiety she almost bumped into a man coming into the agency.

Confused, she heard Patrick say, 'Greg, old son, I'm taking a client out to Bluff Cottage. She's interested in buying. Shouldn't be long.'

'I'll handle it, Lance. No need for you to do it.'

'It's fine. I'd like the break.'

This must be Mr McCann, she thought. Older, navy suit, collar and tie. Typical sales, more reliable than Mr Patrick, yet she said nothing as he turned to her.

'OK, Mrs Lawson? See you shortly out front.'

He disappeared back into the shop.

Penny climbed into her car, more relaxed now that McCann knew Lance Patrick was taking her out to the Bluff. Not that he showed the slightest interest in her as a woman, but you had to be careful these days. In her car, she waited, for what seemed an age. At last she heard a toot behind her, looked into her rear-view mirror and saw the blue Ford ease into the kerb. She waved her hand, signalling she'd seen him. He activated his right-hand turning light and pulled away. She followed.

In fifteen years Sandy Bluff hadn't changed much. This morning she'd indulged herself after she arrived by wandering along the main street. She'd noticed a pleasant, new park, a few craft shops, a motel, a caravan park updated with en-suite cabins. Though she'd brought a picnic lunch, Penny hadn't been able to resist the coffee shop, where she'd ordered a toasted sandwich and a pot of tea. It pleased her that the little town was still undiscovered by the take-away companies and had somehow managed to retain its natural charm, its tidy town image.

Over the bridge, the road led back to Melbourne through an avenue of plain trees, each one dedicated to the memory of a soldier from the area who had died during the First World War. Shelley's great grandfather Stewart's plaque sat beneath one of the trees. When she came back to live here, she'd take Jamie to search it out. They'd polish it together, hug the tree trunk, and remember Shelley. Where was her friend these days? They'd lost touch after Shelley went overseas and stopped writing. Maybe, once Penny moved in, she'd try to locate her.

She could hardly wait to get to the cottage. The excitement, the prospect of living here again, was giving her goose bumps. In front, the blue car turned on to an unmade road. She followed, remembering every twist and turn, as it snaked back across grassland and stunted tea-tree to the ocean. But these days, deeply rutted, water-logged in places after last night's rain, her car bounced around, so she eased off the accelerator. Mr Patrick moved well ahead. If he wanted to treat his car so roughly, let him.

When she pulled her vehicle to a halt outside the cottage, she looked about her, and for the first time saw it with unfettered eyes. Pickets were broken or missing from the fence, long ago its paint had peeled away in most places, the garden was overgrown, the trees bowed and mis-shapen.

The wild winds buffeted her car, and her enthusiasm took a dive. Lonely didn't adequately describe it. This afternoon on the Bluff, everything looked almost forsaken. Was she really thinking of making it her permanent home?

2

When Penny heard him cough, startled, she glanced around her. Lance Patrick leaned against his vehicle, the chest of his shirt ballooning in the howling gale. The man ought to be shivering, cowed by the elements, but not him. He looked so strong, so sure. A rock, she thought. Somehow it gave her confidence, renewed her resolve. If he wasn't fazed by this place, neither was she.

Setting back her shoulders, she reminded herself she'd loved it as a child. She and Shelley used to wrap up against the cold on invigorating walks and at night they'd snuggle up by the fire and play Monopoly or Scrabble. Sometimes they'd read. She would recreate it all for her son. Mr Patrick, she noticed, was tapping his index finger on the car's roof.

He was an odd mixture of indolence

and impatience to get things done. Shrugging, she alighted from her car, pulled on her knitted cap to tame her hair, and wondered why it had suddenly become so important to him that she rent this little cottage? He'd earn very little sales commission on it. Although the thought niggled away in the recesses of her mind, she determined not to allow it to prevent her from pursuing her own campaign.

'What kept you?' he asked as she pitted herself against the wind to reach the gate.

'I own my car,' she shouted, clutching her jacket about her. 'I respect it. Yours probably comes as part of your salary package.'

He grinned, but said nothing. He beat her to the peeling picket gate which hung drunkenly from the top hinge.

'You can see the sign, **For Sale**, can't you?' she gloated.

'I'll take it down before I leave.'

You mean you actually do manual

work, too, she felt tempted to ask. But she had far more important things on her mind than point-scoring. He managed to push the gate ajar without it collapsing.

'Your mansion, Mrs Lawson,' he said, gesturing with his arm.

A sudden gust of wind buffeted her and she stumbled against him. As his hand locked about her arm, she felt its strength, the imprint of warm fingers through her layers of clothing. Glancing up at him, to her dismay she found intense blue eyes studying her. She thought he might draw her closer — silly of her. With hooded eyes, he spoke.

'Lovely, isn't it?'

'Lovely?'

'The house. It's got real potential.'

He had to be teasing. She ventured another glance up at him. His eyes were no longer impatient, but gleaming.

'You mean it was quite beautiful.'

She picked her way, as quickly as she

dared, along the rough, uneven foot-path. Could she afford to risk her small legacy in buying Bluff Cottage? On her earlier visit today she'd only viewed it from the perimeter, thinking someone may be in residence. Now she forced herself to look critically at it, instead of gazing at it with the eyes of a nostalgic schoolgirl.

She saw that, but for the climbing ivy, the rambler roses and the rough poles supporting the veranda, it would have collapsed long ago. She and Shelley had sat out there on long, hot summer holidays, sipping home-made lemonade, reading movie magazines, giggling.

'I didn't realise it was in such bad repair. I think I may have been too enthusiastic,' she said, disappointed.

Lance Patrick shuffled a bunch of keys. He could hear the regret in her voice, but decided she was probably kidding him, pretending she'd lost interest, in order to get the price down to rock bottom. He always had been a pretty suspicious guy. It went with his training. Penelope Lawson was a smart cookie. She was no fool and knew how to use those sure-fire eyes, eyes the colour of dark chocolate. When she'd stumbled against him, he'd smelled the freshness of her in his nostrils, felt the warmth of her beneath his touch. Anyway, he couldn't let her pull out of the arrangement now that he'd set his plan in motion. He had a lot depending on her living here.

'Nonsense, Mrs Lawson. The stone walls are in excellent shape, and the blue slate roof tiles look pretty weather-proof. A rub down and a few coats of paint on the window frames, a clean-up of the paving and garden, and soon we'll have the cottage as good as new. They don't build houses like this any more. Let's take a look inside.'

'My,' she said, 'you are boosting the place up. You don't happen to own it yourself by any chance?'

His stomach knotted. He was being too pushy, behaving as if he were a real salesman. Slow it down, he told himself.

'Look, I'm trying to help you here. I didn't think of the rent option straight off. But you sounded so keen on the place, to tell the truth, I didn't want to disappoint you. If we're wasting our time, however . . . '

'I've come this far, so I might as well look inside.'

Thank goodness, he thought, the place is in fairly good nick inside. He tested his memory. Had anything been left lying around? Anything that might arouse her suspicion? But there was nothing he couldn't explain away if necessary. Over the years, he'd become expert at inventing excuses. Once his job had called for it. He placed a key in the door and it swung open with a groaning sound.

'Well,' he said, stepping aside, 'after you.'

She pushed by him, paused in the hallway and sniffed.

'I thought it might smell a bit musty.'

'It's used as a weekender. I told you that, didn't I?'

Mrs Lawson nodded, and as she took off her cute, knitted cap, her long fair hair bounced about her shoulders. He heard her gasp.

'I can't believe it. It's in such good condition. The same paper on the passage walls, when Shelley's parents had it hung. I loved it. The Regency stripes looked so elegant against the cornices and moulded ceiling roses. It's a bit grotty, but it could be washed down. I can't wait to see the kitchen and bathroom. They're what count. I need plenty of warmth in the kitchen.'

She shivered noticeably. He wished he had a coat to offer her. He'd like to have laid it across her shoulders.

'And you'll get it. I'll see to it, Mrs Lawson.'

There was no denying her velvety smile, its charm, even to a hard-bitten guy like himself.

'Thank you. I'm sorry we got off to a bad start, because really you've been

24

ever so helpful. Even if I can't afford to buy this place, I'm grateful for the chance to see it again. The memories are flooding back. They were wonderful days.'

'You're welcome. Lead on, Mrs L, you obviously know where everything is in the old place.'

He knew every inch of the cottage himself, but he mustn't give that away.

'The kitchen is at the back of the house. It used to have a wonderful slow-combustion stove which operated the oven and the hot water. We spent so much time in front of it during the winters, learning how to cook, and play games. Shelley's mum taught me how to cook. My mother went to work and didn't have the time. I can almost feel the warmth now.'

'Cosy, eh?'

When it came to small talk, Lance didn't usually have the time or the inclination for it. His education was sadly lacking in that department, especially since Carolyn walked out of his life. Now, he wished he'd at least had some recent practice. Penny Lawson probably thought him an inarticulate jerk.

Their feet echoed on the once-polished floorboards, as they passed several rooms opening off the passage-way. The door on one stood closed. She tried the handle, and was about to enter. His inside knotted and his hand closed over hers. If she looked in there, she might start asking awkward questions.

'That's Smithy's room,' he said quickly. 'I forgot to mention, but he said it's in a bit of a state and would you mind not going in. He'll pick up his things this week.'

She looked up at him with dark eyes.

'Mr Patrick, can I have my hand back, please?'

'Sorry.'

Her fingers were gloved, but there had been a special warmth. Lance had to wonder at his reaction.

'I'll lock it for now,' he said, selecting

a key from his ring.

'You don't trust me not to peek?'

It wasn't a matter of trust. Put simply, he couldn't take the risk.

'Some women can't help themselves,' he said with a phoney laugh. 'Lead on.'

He gestured, staying behind her, until she reached the staircase. She glanced up briefly.

'We'll do the attic later,' she said and moved on, her destination clearly the big room at the rear.

The door stood half open. It scraped across the floor as she pushed it aside, and walked into the area. With a thrill of excitement, she hurried across to the large, slow-combustion stove set within a stone chimney.

He stayed in the doorway, halted by an unwelcome thought. He'd forgotten about the stove. No guessing what her next words would be. He needed a plausible answer, and fast. She turned back to him, questions radiating from her dark eyes.

'That's funny. It's still warm. The

stove was lit very recently. Someone's been here, using the house.'

Lance shuffled his feet. From the minute Penny Lawson had stepped into the agency he'd assessed her as bright, not easily taken in. And damn it, if he'd been more obliging, more helpful, he could have had her out of town, and on her way back to Melbourne an hour ago. But no. When she revealed her knowledge of the district, his mind shifted into top gear. He couldn't let her leave until he had more information about her. He'd formulated a plan, a plan that might just work and save him a lot of time and money — a plan he was now committed to.

'The owner was probably here at the weekend.'

She shrugged out of her jacket and hung it over a chair.

'It's Tuesday, not the weekend.'

Her voice had a mocking tone.

'It feels as if someone was here this morning.'

He gestured with open palms.

'Could have been. Smithy didn't mention it, but then he doesn't have to get our permission to stay in his own house. He has a set of keys.'

'You're being supercilious, Mr Patrick. My point is that you should have asked his permission to show me around. What if we'd burst in uninvited?'

'Didn't I tell you? I got permission. I rang after you left the office. You may have noticed I didn't get out to you straight away? I was calling Smithy.'

She nodded.

'So now you're telling me you got permission from this person called Smithy. From now on I'd prefer to do my own negotiating with him. I'd be grateful for his phone number, please.'

'He's not the sort of guy who bothers with a business card. Besides, the agency doesn't give out that kind of information, Mrs L.'

'Would you stop calling me that?'

'Blowed if I'm going to call you Lady Penelope.'

It was the wrong thing to say, but he

couldn't help grinning. Penny almost groaned. Inevitable really that he'd call her that, but it hadn't taken him long to get around to it.

'You're right! I'm Mrs Lawson to you. Do I get the owner's name?'

She watched him move his loose-limbed body, almost gracefully, beneath the low door lintel, cross the room, and join her by the stove. He held his hands to its heat, stalling, he thought.

'Reckon you're right. The stove has been going overnight. Works well, doesn't it? It won't need to be replaced after all. Say, why don't you take off your gloves?'

He had such a friendly grin, one which begged a similar response. Though she knew she couldn't allow herself to be charmed by as little as a friendly grin, her lips curved naturally. She had forgotten she still wore her gloves. She removed them and stuffed them into her pocket.

'Smithy didn't mention he'd been here recently when I talked to him earlier, but if you want an answer, I'll get to the bottom of this.'

Lance Patrick produced a mobile phone from his shirt pocket, tapped in a number, and moved aside. He could have gone to another room if it had been private, so it didn't trouble Penny that she heard his side of the conversation, as she stood, her back to the stove, warming herself.

'It's Lance again, mate,' he began. 'You didn't mention you were here overnight. Yeah, gotcha. OK, makes sense. The young lady and I are looking the place over now. She's set on buying it. You're prepared to pay for the necessary repairs so she can move in immediately? Great! She'll be pleased. I'll give you a bell later with details of the arrangements.'

During the call, Penny had time to look more closely at the kitchen and realise it very definitely had possibilities. She was really fired up again about owning the place, even turned over in her mind the possibility of using part of it to run tea-rooms in the better weather. The really wild southerlies only blew in the depth of winter. For the remainder of the year, the shoreline below the Bluff offered visitors a bracing walk, surfing, fishing, swimming. After today she wouldn't have to deal with Mr Patrick. She'd go direct to the other salesperson, Greg McCann. She filed his name away in her mind.

Patrick replaced his phone, moved back to the stove.

'Just as I thought. Smithy came down yesterday for a few hours fishing with a mate. It was so cold, they lit the stove and spent most of their time playing poker. And the good news is . . .'

'I can rent the place. I heard that much. I have to admit, your way of doing business seems a little strange to me, but I've decided I want this cottage, so I'm taking a chance and going ahead with the arrangements. My terms are a six-month lease with the option of buying after that, the rent to come off the price of the house.'

She put her hands to her hips as if in challenge, though mentally, she had her fingers crossed. He'd never agree to everything.

'You drive a hard bargain but Smithy sounds keen to offload the place. I think I can negotiate a contract under those terms.'

She tilted her head, frowned in disbelief.

'You do?'

He drew a small notebook and pen from his shirt pocket.

'Have you got time to inspect everything, so I can list the things you want done immediately?'

'I'd rather talk to a carpenter who can advise me. There's no need for you to stay. I'll make my own list. I don't want to be hurried by someone breathing down my neck.'

'Sorry if that's what I seem to be doing. I'll get going then. You can phone, or drop the list back at the agency before you leave town. Here's my business card.'

'Thank you.'

Suddenly she felt ungracious. Though he'd done it in an unconventional way, he had managed to get the place for her, and on excellent terms.

'Look, I've got a vacuum flask of tea and some biscuits in the car. Would you join me for a small celebratory drink?'

'I can never turn down a free drink. Can I fetch them from the car?'

Smiling, she handed him her keys.

'Would you mind? You'll find a picnic basket in the boot. I might take a quick look upstairs while you're away. I'm dying to see the attic. Shelley and I used to sleep up there.'

Penny expected to find thick layers of dust on the stairs, but not so. They were dusty, grimy, but the rail was littered with hand-prints, and at the top of the narrow staircase, the door of the attic bedroom stood open. In the gloom she saw the chaos of storage boxes, broken furniture, faded old pictures, a bed, papers. Clearly someone had visited recently, for again there were prints of hands, feet, signs in the dust that things had been lifted, shifted and replaced.

She picked her way through the debris, gasping as she saw the same huge old wardrobe lining the east wall, before making her way to the window which looked southward to the sea. As she dragged the curtains aside, they came apart in her hands. She pulled at them, and together with the rod which held them, they fell to the floor in a cloud of dust. Coughing, she tried to open the window, but it was stuck firmly.

Below, she could see Lance at her car. He appeared to be searching inside. Hadn't she said the basket was in the boot? Perhaps not. Again she tried the window so she could shout to him to look in the boot, but without luck. Getting it to open would figure high on her list of things to do.

As she retraced her steps, she pushed a few boxes aside, made a walkway back to the door, her heart pounding with excitement, wishing she didn't have to return to Melbourne tonight. Soon the cottage would be hers and Jamie's. She longed to get into the task of cleaning up.

Halfway down the stairs, Patrick re-entered the front door, carrying the basket. He looked up at her, his dark hair tousled across his forehead.

'She's blowing a gale out there,' he gasped. 'Discover anything interesting upstairs, Mrs Lawson?'

'Only that I've got a big task ahead of me to clean it up.'

'Will you have any help?'

She shook her head as she continued down the stairs.

'You're too young to be a . . .'

'A widow. I'm used to people saying that,' she interrupted.

His voice softened.

'What happened?'

'A road accident.'

She reached the bottom of the stairs. They stood together outside the kitchen door.

'Don't forget to bob your head,' she

said, needing a change of subject, forcing back the tears.

He stood aside for her.

'Look, I'd be happy to help with the renovations. I'm not bad with the old hammer and nails.'

She swallowed. She didn't know how to respond, so she took the basket from him and led the way into the kitchen. She heard him curse quietly. He was rubbing his head when she looked around.

'You'll have to stop growing,' she said, vaguely cheered by his minor misfortune.

'You spoiled my concentration.'

She decided not to try to understand what he meant, and set to dusting off a place on the large old table with a tea towel from the basket.

'I see you found it.'

'Found what?' he said, sounding startled.

'The basket.'

'Yeah. In the boot, like you said.'

She turned a surprised glance on him.

'So you didn't look in the car?'

A shadow flicked across his eyes.

'Er . . . yes. I noticed you'd left your cheque book on the seat. I put it out of sight. You can't be too careful, even in this lonely spot. Surfie drop-outs hang around a bit.'

'Thanks, that was thoughtful. I tend to be careless about things like that.'

Penny was starting to reassess Lance Patrick. The longer they were together, the more she saw things she liked about him, and felt inclined to accept him. He wasn't everything he claimed, but after the initial hiccup back at the agency, he couldn't have been more helpful. She found herself comparing him with Brad.

Strangely, what she'd loved about her husband when they married, his drive, his purpose, his ambition, had turned sour. He became obsessed with success in the business world, with impressing others, and he became so materialistic. She'd begun to dread the dinner parties she was obliged to give, the one-upmanship of the people who were invited, the social occasions she'd had to attend, not to mention the countless nights she had to leave Jamie in the care of a baby-sitter. In the beginning she'd protested.

'If you want everything,' Brad had said, pointing around their apartment, 'all this, we have to do it.'

He didn't listen when she tried to explain that she didn't want it, that he and his mother wanted it. Eventually the pressure, the pretence, had worn her down. She stopped protesting, and at low moments, drifted into her dreamworld, indulging her yearning for the natural, easy-going life she'd experienced at Sandy Bluff all those years ago. It was always that — a dream, until Brad died so tragically.

'Hey, little lady, where are you?'

Patrick's voice cut through her thoughts. Normally she hated expressions like little lady, but when he said it, his voice had a softness, the lines at the corners of his blue eyes crinkled. She smiled.

'I was thinking about this old cottage, and its potential. There are so many possibilities.'

'Well, I want you to remember what I said before. I'd like to help you clean it up. Time hangs pretty heavy down here during the cold weather, especially when you're living in a motel.'

'I can't believe you don't have a very full diary, Mr Patrick.'

She curved her lips teasingly.

'Could you stretch a point and call me Lance? I hate formality. And my diary is empty, alas. There's not much call for bachelors in these parts. Now about that cuppa.'

'Do you mind drinking from the top of the flask? I only have one mug and I've used it.'

'Not a problem.'

'Milk and sugar?' she asked as she set the lid and her mug on the table, smiling to herself about those fictitious empty diary pages he'd mentioned.

He had the sexy looks, the loose-limbed body, the muscled arms of a man who kept a long list of phone numbers in his little black book. She poured the tea, almost missed her mug, so waylaid was her attention.

'Black and sweet, thanks,' he said.

'Me, too.'

That they had something so ordinary in common pleased her. The sea air was really upsetting her hormonal balance. She almost giggled at the thought. He had pulled two chairs from the table and set them by the stove. Taking one, he stretched long legs lazily in front of him, and folded his hands about the makeshift mug of tea she handed him.

'So what's first on your list? May I call you Pen? Can't get my mouth around Penelope.'

'You just did, and very well.' She laughed. 'As a kid, my classmates used to pronounce it Penny Lope, and my poor mother used to go crazy. But I settle for Penny these days.'

She offered him a tin of melting moments. He took one and bit into it. A crumb fell from his lips, which he caught with his free hand.

'Smashing,' he said.

'You were asking my priorities. First I want the attic cleared out, painted, and the window sash renewed. It will be Jamie's bedroom. I want him to breathe the sea air, have space, let his imagination run free, have secrets.'

She raised an eyebrow and repeated, 'Secrets. What fun for a little kid.'

She's got a child, Lance thought. A little kid could complicate things.

3

The last thing Lance wanted was a nosey little kid hanging around the cottage. He looked hard at Penny though, when he spoke, and tried to sound nonchalant.

'So you've got a son. You haven't mentioned him before.'

Her eyes shone.

'Didn't I? Jamie is the love of my life. He's four. He'll be going to school next year. He's the main reason I've decided to live here. Unfortunately, he has asthma, and I think the clean air will be wonderful for him.'

'Yeah? Me, too. I had asthma as a kid, but not any more.'

She faced him.

'Oh?'

'You can't beat swimming when they're young. It fixed me.'

'That's one of my plans, to get Jamie

lessons at the local pool.'

'I'm afraid it isn't heated, and to do any good, he should swim all year. I'll look around for a private pool for you if you like.'

'You'd do that for me?'

When she looked at him with those soft brown eyes, he had a disturbing feeling he might do almost anything for her.

'I was referring to Jamie's asthma.' He smiled. 'It's not an easy thing for a little guy to handle.'

'You're right, but my head's spinning with ideas to help his breathing. We'll go exploring the rocky outcrops along the shore, we'll invent pirates and smugglers, discover, or at least . . . ' She paused, her face alight. 'As you can see, it doesn't take much to stimulate my imagination. Shelley, the friend I mentioned, and I found a cave. You could only get there when the tide was out, and we . . . '

She held up a hand.

'Here I am burbling on. I'm sure

44

you've got better things to do than listen to my daydreams. I'm getting carried away, boring you.'

'No. I'm in no hurry. Go on.'

He swallowed the last of his tea, waited, hoping she'd continue. She shrugged, stood up.

'Perhaps another time. I should get on the road. I've left Jamie with my mother-in-law. I can't impose on her too late into the evening.'

'But you haven't listed the things you want done before you move in. Would you like to ring your mother-in-law on my mobile and tell her you've been delayed?'

'It's a nice idea, but I think I've seen enough of the house to know I can cope. There are just a couple of things I'd like fixed before I move in. Would I be imposing too much to ask if your agency could arrange them . . . Lance?'

She used his name for the first time, paused first, and dropped her voice when she said it. Either she was using her femininity to try to influence him,

45

or she had begun to trust him. He wished he could be sure. He wondered what she'd think if she knew the truth about him. He wondered if he really wanted to go on with this scheme when a lovely young woman and a small boy were involved.

Lance needed thinking time. Everything was going down too fast. He stood up.

'Sure I can, Penny. Just say the word and I'll have it done.'

'I'd also like the phone connected. I haven't got a mobile. I don't like them much. We never went anywhere as a family without Brad's phone. I know they have their uses, but it always seemed absurd to me that we couldn't have one day without the phone ringing.'

'Business phones can be a real pain, but you'd find one handy down here. I don't think you realise how isolated it can be in winter.'

She looked puzzled.

'What about the big house? A whole

46

community used to live there. Aren't they farming sheep any more?'

'The wool market crashed some years ago and with it went the owners' capital. No-one's lived at Brokenridge for years. The local authorities bought it recently. They want to bulldoze the house and turn the area into a scenic lookout and park. Surfie squatters move in in the better weather and turn it into a bit of a tip. But, as usual, there's the local group of history buffs who want to save it as a tourist thing.'

She shrugged and turned her rich chocolate eyes on him.

'So I'll have some company after all. I'll manage.'

Yes, he thought she would. She had the determination to do anything she set her mind to, which was one of the reasons he'd made that phone call to Andy after she left the agency office.

'I'll organise the phone connections, but it might take a while. Meantime, don't dismiss the idea of a mobile. Now, what was the other thing you wanted me to arrange?' he asked.

'I'd like to have the front and back doors secured. Maybe get the locks changed? That's one risk I'm not prepared to take.'

Behind her smile he read uncertainty, and saw that fragility lay hidden beneath her strength of purpose.

'It's a wise move. Consider it done.'

'I'm glad I bumped into you . . . Lance.'

Again she paused and softened her voice at his name. Again he questioned her purpose. Could it be a stage-managed device to fool him?

'I'm glad, too.'

She reached for her jacket, shrugged into it. He withstood a pressing urge to help her. He stood, observing silently, as she packed the vacuum flask and mugs into the basket. A kind of empty feeling developed inside him, as if he were sorry she was leaving, which didn't make any sense. He'd only known her for a few hours. She handed him the biscuit tin.

'Keep the rest of the melting moments. I'm glad you enjoyed them.'

'Thanks. I'm certainly not going to refuse them. They're much too good. So when might you move in?'

'Hopefully the weekend after next. Our apartment lease runs out in a few weeks, and I don't want to sign another one.'

He whistled. He'd have to get really busy, and go over the place one more time. Once she moved in he wouldn't get the same opportunities.

'That soon? Would you like me to post you the keys to the new locks?'

'Would you? And the bill for your expenses.'

She sounded enthusiastic. He wondered for how long.

'If the contract's ready, my address and phone number are on my husband's business card.'

She handed him a white card with a photograph and embossed printing. Her hand felt soft to his touch and stirred him. It left him uneasy, afraid that without much encouragement he could make a fool of himself with this woman. By then she was on her way to the front door. There, she turned.

'Lance, you remember the terms of our arrangement? A six-month lease, and the rest to be subtracted from the sale price when I buy the cottage. That's what we agreed, isn't it?'

'I haven't forgotten. It's all systems go, Lady Penelope.' He grinned. 'Well, with a name like that, what else can you expect from a guy who was raised on The Thunderbirds?'

She laughed.

'You have the advantage. The only Thunderbird I remember is Brains, and that's hardly an apt name to call you. So, farewell, Mr Patrick.'

'Farewell, Lady Penelope,' he chuckled, and he heard her laugh softly as she closed the front door and was gone.

As if an unknown force were at work, his footsteps led him to the room facing the sea. There, from behind shredded lace curtains, he watched her battle through the gale blowing off the Strait, on her way to the car. If he'd offered to assist her, she would probably have laughed at him and told him not to be patronising. She made it to her car, climbed in, and turned it away from the sea. Soon it disappeared into the distance, and he stood alone.

Lance wiped his brow. Now what? He glanced down at the business card he still held. Mr Bradley J. Lawson had been a good-looking guy, your traditional ambitious yuppie. Lance whistled when he read the address. They lived in one of those flash, high-rise apartments close to the city.

So why would she give up the good life and move to Sandy Bluff? Her story that she wanted clean air for her asthmatic son had some credibility, but she could have afforded a place right on the beach, yet she'd chosen this broken-down little joint. For the memories, she'd said. Maybe, he conceded, she had a secret reason for wanting this particular cottage.

Fifteen or so years had made a lot of difference to this part of the Bluff. Once ancient pens formed barriers from the force of the wind. The Brokenridge Merino sheep grazed the protected inland pastures, and the stately home, its verandas heavy with climbing roses and honeysuckle vines, was built well back from the treacherous Bluff. Then the house and its surrounds rang with sounds of life, of swimming and tennis parties during the lazy summers, charades and chess and banquets during the winters.

Lance had read all about it in a book on local history. He'd wondered why the cottage had been built so close to the Bluff's edge, but the book explained it. The original stone building was first a small lighthouse for ships which plied the rocky coastline. And when Charles Brokenridge took up his land grant in the late eighteen hundreds, he had it extended to become a temporary home for his family when he first brought them out from England. As the sheep industry grew, success came, and Brokenridge built his stately mansion, sited, sensibly, well back from the Bluff.

This really started Lance asking himself again why Penny Lawson thought she could live here happily. He turned the business card over again. If, as she claimed, she truly loved the wide open spaces, how come she'd married a city guy who was a big wheel at one of the major oil companies? Wasn't the simple answer that she'd fallen in love with Mr Bradley J. Lawson? On reflection, maybe it was his bank balance which attracted her, for she hadn't faltered or cried when she mentioned her husband's death, which was just as well, because one thing Lance couldn't handle was a woman in tears. Likely he'd have taken this one in his arms.

He forced his mind back to his dilemma. Her plan to return to Sandy Bluff and her insistence on living at the isolated cottage would be regarded as suspicious, by even the most unsophisticated person. The evidence added up.

She knew the area well. She was about the right age, alone, except for her child, but more telling was the fact that she planned to live out here. There had to be more than a trip down memory lane dragging her back to the cottage.

Talking to her earlier, once or twice things had got a bit sticky, but he'd managed to allay her suspicions with some fancy footwork. He was able to disguise the call he made to his colleague, so it sounded like a call to the owner. But it really got hairy after she challenged him for looking inside her car. Lucky he'd noticed her cheque book on the seat. He'd been careless. That's what the little lady was doing to him, making him lose his concentration, taking his eye off the ball. And that could prove costly. In her presence, he had to be on his toes.

Lance heaved his shoulders and decided to get back to the office before McCann sent out a search party. He killed the fire in the stove, fastened the front door, and stepped out into the wind. He had to go with his instincts, do his real job. The hours were lousy, the pay was lousy, and there were times, like now, when he wished he hadn't agreed to the arrangement. He also wished he didn't have a weakness for women with eyes the colour of hot, melted chocolate.

Penny couldn't believe how fast things moved. Though Brad's mother protested at her taking Jamie so far away, Penny found the strength to remain firm. Alice Lawson almost ran their lives while Brad was alive. She was already halfway to taking over Jamie. If they didn't move away soon, Penny felt she could lose him.

But Alice was helpful in managing to claim most of the apartment furniture. His employers also helped, instructing their solicitors to handle her legal matters, and by paying out the lease for her. Everyone expected Penny to be financially comfortable once her large death benefit insurance was finalised. She told no-one Brad had spent well beyond his income and owed money everywhere. She instructed her solicitor to pay his debts, and after months of legal negotiations, found she was left with enough money to buy a modest home, enough to buy Bluff Cottage.

Though her friends fussed about her leaving, they promised to visit for weekends. She watched them smile at one another, indulge the grieving widow. They didn't say it, but she guessed they were thinking she'd soon return to the city. If they'd known the condition of the cottage they might have laughed aloud.

The keys, as promised by Lance Patrick, arrived in the mail, along with a type-written note on the real estate agency letterhead. Deadlocks had been fitted to both exterior doors, and the phone company had promised a connection as soon as possible. In the meantime, it suggested she should have a mobile. She skipped over the detail and hurried to the signature, Greg McCann, Manager.

Penny had expected Lance to handle things for her. She began to hope he was still around when she moved to Sandy Buff at the weekend, which should have rung alarm bells, but with her new-found independence, she felt a vitality she hadn't had in years.

McCann said Mr Andrew Smith, the owner, hadn't called in to approve and sign the rental contract, but had agreed verbally to her conditions. She shouldn't worry about it, he reassured her. Somehow she trusted Lance and besides, she had more important things to think about.

On Friday morning the removal men arrived to pack and shift the few pieces of furniture she'd decided to keep, because they'd suit the cottage, plus their beds, linen and crockery. By phone, Greg McCann had agreed to open the cottage for them and supervise the unloading. After the van had left, Penny picked up Jamie from kindergarten. At six-o'clock, hand in hand, they went across to an apartment in the same building, to have a farewell dinner with Brad's mother.

There, Penny reluctantly agreed to leave her son with Mrs Lawson over the weekend while she moved into the cottage and made it comfortable. Dust sometimes brought on his asthma, and for the sake of a few days, it was better not to risk it. She hated the thought of going without Jamie, but he loved his gran. She indulged him, particularly since Brad's death. Penny sensed that in Alice Lawson's mind, Jamie was beginning to replace Brad.

It was another of Penny's reasons for putting distance between her child and her mother-in-law. She didn't want him growing up dependent on his gran, expecting her to make things happen if he couldn't do it by himself, believing that money and position were the keys to happiness. Losing Brad had taught Penny a hard lesson. She brushed a tear from her eye. Less than a year ago they were a family, admittedly with a few problems, but they would always have stayed together for Jamie's sake. It took the accident, hers and Jamie's remarkable escape, and the trauma counselling afterwards, to convince her that life was too short to take for granted.

On Friday night the huge, empty apartment echoed with her steps. She tossed and turned on the inflated mattress, before finally getting up and scrounging enough ingredients from the depleted frig and pantry to make a tray of melting moments. When the light of a new day finally filtered through the blinds, Penny stretched, dressed, ate a quick breakfast, and completed her last-minute packing.

Around six in the morning, she closed the door of the apartment, and refusing to look back, made her way to the underground carpark. Unlocking the car, she added her overnight things to the already packed food supplies and clothing, and placed the tin of melting moments on the front seat.

Strange how her mind kept coming

back to those shortbread biscuits. How clearly she could recall Lance's mouth, remembering a crumb which escaped from his lips, and the long, lean fingers which caught it. Would he be exactly as she remembered? She hoped so. She liked his laidback style, even his impatient blue eyes. He got things done. He'd called himself a bachelor. Her heart skipped a beat. She liked that idea, too.

Penny drove through the early-morning traffic towards the Prince's Highway. On the radio the weather bureau forecaster said, 'To the west, the cloud will clear around noon. Expect a few sunny breaks in the afternoon before the showers set in.'

In the three hours the journey took she didn't stop once, and as she turned off the highway on to the road to the Bluff, when she should have slowed, she didn't, not until the tin of melting moments crashed from the seat to the floor of the car. She left them there, but for the remainder of the journey, she kept the speed to a sensible level.

On her earlier visit she hadn't noticed the big house. Now she looked to the east, across the grasslands, and found it stark, crumbling, eerie in the overcast light, surrounded by pines and leafless poplars, stretching upwards like skeletal fingers in prayer. Brokenridge was on its way to haunted status, she thought with amusement. She and Jamie would have such fun exploring the ruins. She'd tell him about the day she and Shelley climbed one of the trees overlooking the garden and were caught, watching the rich at play.

Around the next turn her cottage came into view — her cottage. She sighed with pleasure, and as if to respond, a beam of sunshine pushed clouds aside and settled over the land. What a wonderful welcome. She pulled the car alongside the picket fence and reached for her binoculars in the glove box. It wasn't until the afternoons that the ocean winds turned their full fury upon the Bluff. Though the sun stayed only a short time, the morning was comparatively calm. At the cliff face, she breathed deeply before putting the glasses to her eyes. She searched for the track she and Shelley had used to get down to their cave at low tide. Before she introduced Jamie to it, she wanted to do the climb alone to make sure it was safe.

She realised now, as she focused on the slope, it was more a track, than the strategically placed rocky outcrops which she had in her mind. Then she noticed the rusting iron ribs of a shipwrecked vessel. Penny had quite forgotten it. She and Shelley used to romanticise about the young couple who, it was rumoured, had fallen in love on their way out from England, staggered ashore from the shipwreck and died in each other's arms.

Suddenly the wind picked up, she shivered, sensing danger, for she was much too close to the edge. Gulls shrieked overhead, and as she stepped back, a pebble gave way beneath her foot, and she stumbled forward.

Dear heaven, had someone tried to push her?

4

Penny was falling. She screamed as she fought to regain her footing.

Then out of nowhere, strong arms wrapped about her, dragging her back from the edge. Turning, her breath coming in short gasps, she looked into Lance Patrick's blue eyes, and threw herself into his arms.

'I was scared . . . so scared,' she cried out against his chest. 'I thought I was being . . . '

'Hush, you're safe now. You panicked. It's OK.'

He brushed her hair back from her face.

'You were far too close to the edge. Didn't I warn you how dangerous it is up here, especially as the winds pick up?'

'I know. I didn't think I was that close, and then . . . I must have imagined it, but I thought someone pushed me.'

He stared down at her, and then placed her at arm's length.

'You do have quite an imagination, Penny. I'd say the wind caught at the back of your jacket.'

Penny suddenly felt foolish at letting her emotions run out of control, and falling into his arms like a scared rabbit. She dragged herself from his hold.

'Anyway,' she snapped, 'what are you doing here?'

'And a very good morning to you, too. It's so nice to see you again, Lady Penelope.'

She couldn't resist his smile, couldn't deny her pleasure at seeing him, but, still shaky, neither could she bring herself to admit it.

'I wasn't expecting you. You didn't have to come. I have my own keys. Mr McCann sent them to me.'

'I called by with the paint you asked Greg to arrange.'

'I don't understand why you're being so helpful.'

'I enjoy it. I've got nothing better to

do. You're on your own. Are they reasons enough? Besides, I promised I'd give you a hand, and a promise is a promise.'

Lost for a suitable response, Penny kept walking towards the cottage. As the track dipped away, the wind's intensity eased slightly. She noted how he shortened his stride so as not to leave her behind. She searched for something ordinary to say. Finally, he spoke.

'You're not going to like this either, but I've taken the liberty of getting the stove going. It's lovely and warm inside.'

In her present ambivalent mood, Penny stopped short. She'd been taught never to look a gift horse in the mouth, and a warm house sounded very inviting, but really . . .

'Who let you in?' she asked abruptly.

'I did.'

He looked straight ahead.

'So there's a spare set of keys to my cottage floating around in your pocket?'

'Of course. The agency has a set of keys. How did you expect the furniture people to get in? I was trying to be helpful.'

Penny was out of answers. The uncomfortable silence between them resumed. Her thoughts were just as mixed up and uncomfortable. When they reached the cottage fence, the picket gate swung open at his touch. It had been repaired, painted and looked as new.

'I suppose you did this, too?'

'Guilty as charged.'

He didn't sound as if he felt guilty, not at all, and the irony was, she did, for not saying thanks. But he was crowding her, taking over in a way, and hadn't she come here for freedom from bossy, managing people? She moved towards the front door.

'I'm glad you didn't touch the garden. I'm looking forward to doing that myself.'

His blue eyes glittered with amusement as he looked around at what was more than a rambling garden. Penny guessed he thought she couldn't do it alone, which made her stiffen her back with determination.

'Where's your little fella? I was hoping to meet him,' he asked as they approached the door.

'He's not coming down until next week.'

'You'll be here alone over the weekend? Is that a good idea?'

'Are you trying to scare me, Mr Patrick?'

'It looks like we're back to square one, Lady Penelope Lawson.'

Again he drew a smile to her lips, repentance to her heart.

'OK, I admit I'm behaving badly. It's just that I imagined things happening differently.'

'What do you mean?'

'Somehow I envisaged I'd be alone, place my shiny new key in the door lock, turn it, and walk over the threshold, and into a new life.'

She laughed shakily.

'And here I am getting in your way. OK, I'll see you inside and then I'm out of here.'

Penny blushed. She had no idea what to say. Part of her found him interesting, attractive, pleasant to be with, part of her wanted him to stay.

He swung open the door. The hall looked brighter. The papered walls had been washed down, the overhead light cord repaired. Someone had placed the grandfather clock, inherited from her parents, between the two bedroom doors, the position exactly right. When she and Brad had moved into their new apartment, he'd insisted it didn't fit the contemporary decor, and consigned it to her workroom. It hadn't been worth another argument, for arguments, even minor ones, upset Jamie, and sometimes triggered an asthma attack.

Penny turned gratefully to Lance. He'd retreated to the veranda's edge. The wind rustled through his hair, settling it wildly across his forehead. Maybe she imagined the loneliness in his blue eyes, but whatever, it reminded her she'd been ungracious, ungrateful and undeserving of his help.

'Give me a bell if you need anything. I'm holed up at the Seahorse Motel,' he said.

Her heart reached out to him. She couldn't let him go back to a cold, impersonal motel room.

'Please, Lance, come in. I haven't thanked you properly.'

'It's not necessary. You've already made the point. You need space.'

'There'll be plenty of that once I've settled in. I brought some melting moments.'

She smiled, raised an enquiring eyebrow.

'So you're not above a bit of bribery, eh?'

'Like everyone, I have weaknesses. If the fire's going we can boil a kettle, and I'll make some sandwiches. Perhaps you could help me in with the food and frig boxes from the car?'

To her surprise, her enthusiasm grew.

Soon Penny was busy at the kitchen table cutting sandwiches.

'That's everything,' Lance said as he dumped the last box on the floor. 'I hope you're happy with the way I positioned your furniture. Let me know if you want anything shifted.'

'You arranged the furniture, too? But I asked Mr McCann . . . '

'I volunteered. I should point out there's quite a mess up in that attic. I know you want it for the little guy, but it needs a thorough clean and paint job before anyone can sleep in there. Smithy came around and cleaned his stuff out of the room he occupied, so I thought it might suit Jamie until the attic's finished. I managed to get the window up, air the place off, but you'll have to call a carpenter to fix it permanently.'

'That's wonderful. I can't believe you're doing all this for me.'

She placed sandwiches on two plates, before responding to the whistling kettle. Lance should have been prepared with an answer but he fluffed his lines.

'My . . . er . . . my mother was a widow. I know she needed help, and . . . she hated asking for it. I reckon you're the same.'

He took a sandwich and bit into it.

'They're good. I didn't realise I was so hungry.'

'I bet you don't look after yourself. You probably eat all the wrong foods,' she said quietly. 'Men on their own usually do.'

He glanced down at his stomach.

'Too much weight?'

'No, you look in excellent shape.'

'There's a small gym attached to the local swimming pool.'

He reached for another sandwich, pushing aside the urge to offer to introduce her to the leisure centre. Time enough for that.

'After I've finished my cup of tea, I'll leave you in peace. What are your plans?'

'This afternoon I'll start the big clean up, especially the attic.'

Her eyes caught his glance. He was

probably fooling himself, but he thought she was asking for his help. He almost offered, but didn't.

'And tomorrow I'm taking time off in the morning to find that cave I told you about.'

'That shouldn't be too hard.'

'The area used to be littered with little caverns. Ours was big enough to walk into.'

'You were kids then. It might be a hands-and-knees job now.'

'It had height, though you'd probably have to crawl.'

'Look, I know I keep sounding like your typical macho male, but let me come with you. Have you forgotten what happened a few hours ago? You nearly went over the edge. You know how treacherous the cliffs are in winter.'

She shook her head.

'Only a fool doesn't learn from experience. I'll be careful. But this is something I have to do on my own.'

Lance's stomach knotted. He didn't want Penny involved in his assignment, but the things she said, like just now, seemed to implicate her. Why did she have to be alone on the cliffs? Could she be meeting someone? Searching for something? Signalling someone? It was all suspicion, supposition, guesswork. Lance Patrick damned the fact that he was an expert in all three. Trust? It didn't come easy in his real job.

She was still speaking.

'But after lunch, if you can spare the time, I'd be glad of some help upstairs sorting things out.'

He drank the last of his tea, considering her request. He already knew there was nothing to interest him upstairs. He'd given it another thorough work-over during the week, and he'd fallen behind with his paper work. But why waste time thinking about it? He was always going to agree. Her smile could persuade a crocodile to turn vegetarian!

'Consider it done.'

'Are you from the city, Lance?' she asked.

'Not likely. I was born in a town, inland from here. My parents farmed. I went to boarding school in Geelong and hated it. I reckoned I was a real tough guy. Anyway, much to my parents' disgust, I dropped out in the final year and found a job in the . . . er . . . electronics industry.'

'And you've never married?'

'No. My lady didn't appreciate the hours I spent at work, or the pay packet. I was wasting my life, she said. I think she had a point.'

'Your lady?'

'It didn't get beyond that. Carolyn knew I couldn't offer her what she wanted in life — position, money. They're important to classy women.'

'Some women,' she murmured. 'Come on. If you've finished eating, we've got work to do.'

It was already dark when they finally decided to quit the attic. Penny, in front of him on the stairs, laughed as she pulled off the protective scarf she wore about her head, and shook out her fair hair. It fell to her shoulders, close enough for Lance to reach out and touch its silkiness as it ran through his hands. Working together in that confined space had been tough. He'd kept glancing at her, wanting to hold her. She turned back to him. He was so close at her heels, she unbalanced them both.

'Oops,' she said, her arms reaching for him as she sought to steady herself.

'Any time.'

He grinned. She pulled away. He had to subdue an urge to take her in his arms.

'You've been wonderful. Thanks for helping sort through everything. I feel as if we've made some headway.'

As she hurried down the stairs, he noted the way she said we've. By default, she'd included him. She'd begun to trust him, which was the purpose of the exercise, but it didn't sit well with his feelings about her. He spoke quickly, trying to forget.

'Andy Smith inherited all that stuff

with the house. It probably belonged to the family you used to stay with. He said to keep anything you want, throw out the junk, and any recycled things can be given to a charity.'

He followed her, but at a slower rate, creating distance between them.

'I noticed you've put some toys in a box. Why don't you keep them for your little bloke? They can be scrubbed up.'

'He's over-loaded with toys, thanks to his gran. But I've rescued a teddy bear. I seem to remember it belonged to Shelley. I might clean it up and get it a new eye.'

She laughed again, musical, happy. It didn't take much to persuade him to stay on for dinner. Penny made omelettes and a simple salad, while Lance volunteered to chop wood. He stacked it under the veranda, filled the fireside basket and stoked the stove. He wiped beads of perspiration from his forehead, rinsed his hands under the kitchen sink, and conscious that she watched him intently, tried not to get drawn in by her dark eyes.

They ate sitting opposite one another at the table. Lance forced himself to concentrate on the food, and not on his companion. The cheese and chive omelette tasted delicious.

'It sure beats a diet of pizza and fish and chips,' he told her.

She smiled. His hunger turned to a longing to kiss her. The best advice you can give yourself is to beat a quick retreat out of here, he told himself. But against his better judgment, he hung around, pulling two comfortable chairs to the stove. His home for the last few weeks had been four walls, a bed and a television set, and he'd grown weary of it.

She tried to stifle a yawn.

'When's the rain due?' she asked.

'Any time.'

He forced himself from his chair.

'I should be on my way. Did you hire that mobile phone by the way?'

'I decided to do without a phone until the company can connect one.'

'It could take weeks.'

'I'll hurry them up,' she said.

He laughed.

'By phone?'

She nodded, amusement curving her lips.

'Penny, you're dealing with a big organisation. They don't jump, even when a pretty lady flashes her pearly whites at them. Don't take this the wrong way, but I took the liberty of hiring one for you. I'm uneasy about you being out here alone. I want you to ring me any time, day or night. Don't go anywhere without letting me know.'

He placed the small black instrument casually on the table and moved towards the door. As he expected, irritation stormed into her eyes.

'You have to be joking, Lance.'

He decided to get out before she threw the thing at him. He could guess what she was thinking, but at the door he paused, risking her ire even more.

'While you're out walking tomorrow, I'll pick up those boxes you earmarked for the tip and dump them, if you like.'

'When are you going to stop interfering in my life?' she snapped, following him to the door. 'Don't you listen to a word I say? I don't like mobiles.'

'Give your little guy a call on the phone. You'll feel better after you've talked to him. I'll bet you're missing him already.'

'You're the only one spoiling how I feel. I . . . '

He tugged open the door, stepped into the darkness, and ran to his car. He lost the rest of her reply in the wind, but he didn't need to hear it anyway. He knew it wouldn't be complimentary!

5

Penny clutched at the door as she watched Lance disappear into the black of the night. She was trying to manage her life, make her own decisions, be her own person, and getting there, until Lance Patrick, who thrived on doing things his way, arrived uninvited. Yet, without his assistance today, unpacking, helping with the cleaning, chopping wood, she'd have been sitting in front of an electric fire, wrapped in layers of woollies and a doona, reminded of how cold and tired she felt by the chaos around her.

Back by the stove, she consigned her worthy principle about mobiles to the back burner, picked up the instrument and dialled her mother-in-law's number. After speaking to Jamie, she yawned. Tonight she would not take her uncertainties about Lance to bed. She would sleep. Tomorrow was another day. She could handle the man with the impatient blue eyes.

Penny woke to the shrieking of gulls and the tapping of a tree limb against the window pane. She shivered as she realised she'd forgotten to stoke the stove last night, and flinging on her warm gown, hurried into the kitchen to refuel it. She almost expected to see Lance there doing it for her. Hadn't that been the pattern so far? She chuckled as she placed some wood on the stove to encourage the embers into flames. He'd been her genie. If she rubbed the teapot, he might appear now. Supposing he did, and granted her three wishes. What would they be? Easy. Happiness, freedom, and . . . the third wish stumped her, but in her heart she admitted impatient blue eyes figured somewhere.

She turned on the radio, made breakfast but delayed a shower until she was sure the water had heated.

'Expect overcast but fine weather this

morning. Showers will sweep over the Bluff later today,' the local weather report said.

That, and the early afternoon high tide, moved her to action. Penny set out for the climb down the Bluff to the beach wearing stout walking shoes, a thick, roll-neck sweater, woollen slacks, a parka and gloves. She hung her binoculars around her neck, and pulled the hood over her hair as she leaned into the wind. Without much difficulty she found the opening to the track. It had obviously been used regularly, by surfers she guessed, and she negotiated it more easily than she'd expected.

Halfway down, a narrower path branched off to the left. Hers and Shelley's cave lay along this route. It could be rough, but she was fit, and after yesterday, not inclined to take risks. She'd go a few paces and test it. Soon she'd know if Shelley had ever returned to the cave, as they'd planned all those summers ago, and left her a message. A shiver of expectation ran through her.

The rocky path gave way to firm sand, but when Penny reached the entrance to the cave, her expectations turned to disappointment. It no longer belonged to her youth. It now belonged to people who lit fires and trashed the place. Food scraps, tins, bottles and plastic wrap had taken it over. The aura of magic and mystery had gone. She flopped on to the cave's sandy edge, breathless from the climb. With her index finger she wrote Jamie's name in the coarse granules, then Shelley's, though she had arrived too late to reclaim the territory. Then she stood up and gazed out to sea. The fabulous view remained. No-one could take that away.

A large container ship appeared to sit on the horizon. Closer, crested terns dive-bombed the ocean and feasted on unsuspecting fish. She put her binoculars to her eyes to enjoy their aerobatics, and stood fascinated for sometime. Then, swinging her glasses across the sparkling sea, she searched for the remains of the Longford, wrecked all those years ago. But the tide was coming in. She'd have to bring Jamie earlier in the morning.

Suddenly, she shivered. A stillness, a silence, an eerie sense that someone was nearby swept over her. She shortened the focus on her glasses, searched the cliff face, and then the sand below. If someone was there, and they didn't retreat soon, they could be trapped by the rising tide, which reminded her not to linger herself. She still had her mission to complete.

Her head bent, she entered the cave, and beyond the cold ashes of a previous fire, she worked her way towards the rocky area which flattened out into a ledge. Once, at the back of it, had been a sandy patch, and there, she and her friend had buried their bottle. As she forced herself over the ledge, she gashed her hand, not badly, but enough to leave a rash of angry red lines across its palm. She wrapped it in several tissues from her pocket and went on.

At last she located the sand and with her uninjured hand, burrowed into it. But after ten minutes of searching, she was forced to the conclusion that there was no bottle. Someone had removed it. Not Shelley, for in their plan, she would have left another message. She shrugged. Oh, well, it would be fun to reinvent the idea with Jamie. It would stimulate his imagination. Crouching, she eased herself back to the cave entrance, stretched her limbs outside, and took a last look through her binoculars.

What was that? She blinked and adjusted the lens. Yes, Lance Patrick was picking his way with confident steps across a stony outcrop to higher land. It must have been Patrick down here earlier. A rush of annoyance surged through Penny. Was he keeping a patronising eye out for her, but then she had a more troubling thought. Suppose he had her under surveillance. Her husband and his mother often used to tell her she was naïve, too trusting. How right they were.

She'd accepted Lance into her home, accepted his help, obligated herself to him, yet she knew almost nothing about him. What a fool. Why hadn't she questioned, really tested herself, and demanded credible answers. Why would a personable bachelor be interested in a widow with a small child, and only enough money to buy a run-down property like Bluff Cottage? Yet, from the moment she'd stepped into the estate agency and declared an interest in Bluff Cottage, he'd been at her side, questioning her movements, settling her in, being her right hand. And then her mind connected with another unnerving thought. Suppose he'd been searching her car when she saw him looking through it on that earlier visit?

Searching for what? Keeping her under surveillance for what reason? For the first time she forced herself to confront the doubts swirling around in her head. She had wanted to believe his attention flowed from a growing friendship, a compatibility which they found in one another's company. Loneliness could make you believe in fairies, in dreams. She laughed with disgust. The wind tossed the harsh sound to the sea.

Penny stiffened her shoulders, and with them her resolve, and set out on the route back, determined to discover the real reason for Patrick's interest in her. Her days of being naïve were over. The climb back to the edge of the Bluff took all Penny's energy. Her scratched hand ached, the gathering wind impeded her progress, but once on firm ground, she glanced quickly over the rocks and the shoreline. There was no sign of Patrick. In her present mood she could almost wish he had been caught by the incoming tide which now lapped the lower part of the Bluff.

Back at the cottage, Penny bathed her hand and had a quick snack, before calling Mrs Lawson on the mobile. Wishing it wasn't necessary, she arranged for Jamie to stay until mid-week.

'It's taking me longer to get things sorted. I wouldn't worry, but it's the dust, and Jamie's asthma,' she explained.

Alice Lawson clucked.

'Didn't I tell you, Penny, dear? But you young people always know best.'

Her mother-in-law's words thoroughly ticked her off, and her mood didn't improve when she noticed the boxes of rubbish to go to the council tip had been collected from the back veranda. Lance Patrick had been here during her absence. If he arrived this afternoon, she's really give him the third degree, insist on knowing what he was up to.

Though she busied herself through the afternoon, washing down the kitchen walls, lining the cupboards, organising the pantry, measuring the window for new curtains, she found time to make a pot of vegetable and barley soup. Yet the hours seemed to pass so slowly. It was as if she was waiting for something to happen. Not until she took a melting moment from the cake tin to have with a late cup of tea did she finally admit she'd been waiting for Lance, listening for his voice, hoping to see his loose-limbed frame bob beneath the door lintel as he came into the kitchen.

Except for last night, today was the first time she'd been alone in the cottage. Face it, she said, as she refilled the kettle, you've allowed yourself to be taken in by the man. If your mother-in-law knew, heaven forbid the tuttutting, the patronising lectures, the charge of being an unsuitable mother. Damn it all, if I'm attracted to a man, that means I'm a normal thirty-year-old, she told herself, as she took up a wooden spoon and stirred the soup. Ladling out a little, she tasted it. Lovely, she thought.

She hadn't made soup since they'd shifted into the South Yarra apartment.

Brad didn't want her wasting time on something as down-to-earth as home-made vegetable soup. He wanted her at charity afternoon teas. Penny smiled. She knew someone who would appreciate a bowl of home-made soup, someone who enjoyed home cooking. Should she risk it? Wouldn't it be better to forget Mr Patrick altogether? That's what her mother-in-law would have said in far more direct language.

She reached for the phone. She had a bone or two to pick with Mr Patrick anyway. Why had he followed her this morning? Could she find out without arousing his suspicions?

Lance pulled his car into the parking bay outside his motel room. The drizzling rain had begun half an hour ago. It would probably go on for most of the afternoon. A package of fish and chips under one arm, he opened the door of his room and heaved a huge sigh. He hated this dreary existence, longed to get back to his farm. The sooner he cleared up this matter, the sooner he could start living a normal life again.

But normal was no longer what it had been last week. He'd met Penny. He shrugged off his damp anorak, turned on the heater, and stabbed at the television button. Footballers' images grew, cheering crowds filled the small room. Cheering was the last thing he felt like, but he needed background noise to ease the isolation, the loneliness, the trend of his thoughts. As he picked at the fish, played with the unappetising chips, he wondered why, these days, they always smelled so much better than they tasted.

The football match failed to grab his attention. His mind took a one-way path back to the widow at Bluff Cottage. He didn't want her to be the person he was after. Only circumstantial evidence pointed to her anyway, and now he felt ninety-nine-point-nine per cent sure she was what she seemed — a young widow making a fresh start. The fact that she'd sought out the cottage had to be a coincidence. This morning's events had strengthened that assessment.

After taking the rubbish from her attic to the dumping station, surreptitiously he'd searched her out on the cliffs, and found her easily. You couldn't miss the red parka, hardly the colour of garment you'd wear if you were trying to fade into the environment. She'd done nothing suspicious, unless you wanted to get paranoid about the fact that she'd spent sometime with her binoculars looking out to sea. The cave she'd visited held nothing of interest for him. He'd been through it, as he had her attic, several times, but found nothing to arouse his suspicions.

Following his surveillance, he'd reported in to his colleague, Andy Smith.

'We're wasting our time with her,' he'd said. 'I vote we eliminate her from our enquiries.'

But he'd known Andy wouldn't agree. Earlier, he'd made the mistake of confiding in his colleague.

'You should see her. She's got these eyes the colour of hot, dark chocolate and long fair hair.'

Today he paid for letting his feelings loosen his tongue.

'Mate, don't go falling for the little widow. They're always the worst, the helpless, innocent-looking ones with the big eyes. Get your mind on the job, son. Stick with her another week or two. It could be crucial.'

Another week or two? Could he do that with a clear conscience? He bundled up the cold remains of the fish and chips and hurried through the rain to an outside bin to dispose of them. He groaned as he re-entered his room. A laptop and paperwork glared at him from the makeshift desk he'd set up. As he rinsed his hands, he noticed as he glanced in the mirror, the letters sticking out of his shirt pocket. He'd found them amongst the attic rubbish when he'd been disposing of it. With no more than a quick glance, he'd plucked them from the litter and shoved them in his shirt pocket, planning to read them later. At the table, he pulled out the first, flattened it, ran his handkerchief over it to remove some of the surface grime.

The envelope was addressed to the last owner of the cottage, Mrs Edith Anderson, whom he knew to be Penny's friend's mother. He drew the letter from the envelope. It was no more than correspondence dated more than twelve years ago, from an elderly aunt, happy they were coming to live in the city. He tossed it into the bin.

Cheering from the television set captured his attention. Somebody had scored a goal. The umpire waved two flags. The scores flashed on to the screen. It was a close match. Lance got involved. He crossed to the bed, dropped on to it, and, propping himself up with pillows, his attention captured, watched, occasionally shouting instructions to the players. But half the game later, his eyelids drooped. He placed his arms behind his head and sank down into the bed.

The phone rang. In a fog of weariness, he groped for the handset.

'Yeah? Patrick,' he said sleepily.

'Er ... is that you, Lance? It's Penny.'

She sounded tentative. Suddenly he was awake.

'Penny, what's wrong?'

She laughed, her happy laugh.

'Nothing. Should there be?'

'So why are you calling?' he growled.

'If you're going to be like that ... '

'Come on, Pen. Stop mucking around. I'm not in the mood. Are you OK?'

'I've made a pot of vegetable soup, there's no-one here to help me eat it, and since you're the only person I know in these parts, I thought ... '

In the background more cheering erupted.

'Oh, I'm sorry. You've obviously got people there.'

'My best friend, the telly. The Western Bulldogs have just scored the winning goal.'

And so have I, he thought, raising his brows, an invitation to the widow's cottage. His first.

'Then you wouldn't mind some company? Will you join me for dinner?'

'I'm not about to turn down home-made soup with a lovely lady. Pity the bakery is closed on Sunday afternoons. I could have picked up some of their crusty rolls.'

'And ignored mine?'

'Home-made bread, too? I'm on my way.'

It took less than thirty minutes for him to shower, change into a clean shirt and jeans. Pulling on a thick polo-necked sweater and his anorak, he was on the road, heading for Bluff Cottage, wishing he had a bottle of red wine he could contribute, wishing it was a real, romantic date.

Red alert. SOS. You're on the job, mate. Get your mind into gear. Andy's voice filtered through his thoughts.

The drizzling rain had stopped by the time he made it to the cottage. Though he still had a key to Penny's property, he was too well-trained to risk antagonising her by using it. He'd had it cut by arrangement with the estate agency manager. Under pressure from police headquarters, Greg McCann had agreed to co-operate, and allow Lance to masquerade as a property salesman with an interest in computer systems. Though Greg received no briefing, he'd already indicated he suspected Lance was attached to the drug squad, which was wrong, but suited their purposes, for if McCann were tempted to confide their presence to anyone in the local community, his theory would be accepted. These days people knew that the vast Australian coastline tempted drug traffickers of every substance.

Lance went around to the back entrance. The door was unlocked.

'Hello, Penny, it's Lance,' he called.

'Come in, if you're good-looking.'

'I'd better go home then.'

'Come in anyway. I can stand it if you can.'

He hurried in, almost forgetting to lower his head, sniffing the air.

'Mmm. Something smells awfully good.'

Penny's gaze caught smiling eyes, dark, unruly hair in her quick glance, as he entered, and she knew it had been a mistake to invite him.

'Awfully good,' she said. 'Isn't that a contradiction in terms?'

She thought how awfully good he looked! And when he smiled, and nodded, acknowledging her correctness, her heartbeat broke into a wild rhythm. These days Penny's thoughts didn't make a lot of sense to her, but she did know that she'd grown tired of polished manners and correct English, and Lance brought a freshness, a freedom and an exciting uncertainty into her life. He stretched to his full height.

'If I'm going to be coming around so often, you might need to have your door lintels raised.'

'Sit down and warm yourself. Excuse

me while I prepare a pasta dish to follow the soup. And I'll talk to the carpenter about the doors when he comes to fix the window sashes.'

'You don't have to go to that expense. I was kidding. So did you sleep well last night? Get any painting done today?'

He looked uncomfortable, standing in the middle of the room, as if he needed something to do.

'Yes, and no.'

She pulled out the cutlery drawer in the table.

'Since you're not sitting down, make yourself useful and set the table. Yes, I slept well.'

'But you didn't do any painting. So how did you spend the day?'

He kept his eyes on his task.

Penny almost said, 'I think you know how I spent the morning,' but when she questioned him about this morning, she wanted it to be more subtle than that. She decided to save it until after they'd eaten. No point in spoiling the meal.

Instead she gestured with her hands.

'I've been slaving away here in the kitchen and you can't even see the difference?'

He nodded.

'You've hurt your hand.'

He strode to her side.

'It's nothing, just a scratch.'

He reached for it. She avoided his touch by using the injured hand to pick up a peeler.

'So how about you? What have you been up to?'

'Nothing much,' he said shortly.

'That tells me a lot.'

Her heart had stopped pounding. He's hedging, she thought, but later she'd drag the truth out of him.

'So, you've relented. You used the mobile after all. Sensible girl.'

Now he was changing the subject. He sounded vaguely patronising, but she left it.

'You were right, of course. I need a phone. I rang Jamie last night and again today.'

She smiled.

'And me this afternoon.'

The cutlery clattered as he laid it on the table.

'And you,' she said and kept stirring the sauce.

'I'm looking forward to meeting your little guy. Did you say you were going back to town to get him tomorrow?'

'No, I didn't say.'

The minute she replied she knew she'd been too abrupt. Would he sense she was holding back information on her movements?

'Oh? So when's he coming?'

'During the week. I want to get the attic painted and aired out first. Shall we eat?'

He laughed.

'You're asking me?'

She ladled the soup into two bowls and invited him to cut the bread.

'Listen, Penny, after the meal, why don't we paint the attic? We could do it over in a few hours. You must be longing to have young Jamie with you.'

Penny drew in her breath. Could

they, she wondered, as she stared at the man who kept her mind churning over and over with uncertainty. But he avoided her eyes as he took a spoonful of the soup.

'I miss him terribly. But I couldn't ask you to . . . ' she began.

'I'm offering, Lady Penelope.'

He concentrated on his soup, but there was laughter in his voice.

'This is good, delicious.'

Penny tackled her soup, too, but struggled with competing emotions. If she could get Jamie's room painted tonight she could bring him home tomorrow. But could she accept help from a man who stirred her heart, but whose conduct sometimes troubled her? Better to deal first with her doubts. She'd do that at the end of the meal.

Penny served the pasta, offered the salad, and kept the conversation light, concentrating it on the changes to Sandy Bluff and the local facilities and schools. For coffee, they settled on the old cottage sofa, which Penny had had dry cleaned, draped with a sheet and placed to one side of the stove. Now she would tackle him about this morning. She began, the sentences worked out in advance.

'Lance, on my walk this morning, I noticed you down on the rocks. You didn't mention you'd gone for a walk earlier.'

'Yeah, that's right. You saw me, eh? I usually take a morning stroll along the beach if the weather's fine.'

'I wondered at the time if you were keeping a check on me.'

He glanced quickly up at her, attempted a laugh.

'You've caught me out. Yes, I was keeping an eye on you. I was worried about you climbing over that Bluff. I know its dangers, and I couldn't forget you almost fell yesterday.'

'So you were following me? Why?' she demanded.

'Hey, Pen.' He moved closer. 'Why so serious? I called at the cottage first. You weren't here, so I picked up the rubbish and shot that down to the dump. When you hadn't returned to the cottage when I got back, I started to worry. I know you didn't want me around, but I went down to the Bluff in case something had happened to you.'

Penny edged away from him. Too easily he set her heart alight, clouded her judgment.

'So why didn't you let me know you were around? I began to think you had me under surveillance. Why? I didn't have a clue.'

He put his coffee mug to his lips. She waited. Would those full, sensuous lips lie?

'If I'd let you know I was around, you'd have got mad at me.'

He placed his cup on the low table, took her chin in his strong hand, forced her to look into his eyes.

'Now wouldn't you?'

'I certainly would have. You don't seem to take a bit of notice of anything I say. I'd appreciate it if in future you did.'

'You're such a little thing. You invite offers of help.'

She tilted her chin.

'I am not helpless.'

'You think I don't know that? You're a gutsy woman. But when I look at you . . . oh, enough said. Now what about that painting? Are you up to it?'

Penny's mind worked overtime, so did her heart. He was telling her something her heart wanted her to hear, her mind to reject. Her mind told her something else. She couldn't spend the remainder of the evening so close to him, and the sooner Jamie came home . . .

'If you're sure you don't mind. It would be good to make a start.'

He stood up, as if he, too, were anxious to escape the intimacy they shared on the sofa.

'What are you waiting for? Chop, chop, Lady Penelope.'

In three hours they covered the ceiling, beams and walls, painting out the drabness with an off-white colour.

Penny stood in the doorway and inspected their work. A second coat, and a finishing semi-gloss with a hint of sunshine in its colour, for the window and door frames, and the room would look superb.

'Should we close the window over-night?' Lance asked, as he stood beside her.

'No, the cool air will help dispel the odour. I keep it open anyway. I'll finish the painting tomorrow, and on Tuesday I'll bring Jamie to his new home. Lance, I'm so looking forward to that. Starting our new adventure together.'

The soft pad of his finger grazed her cheek. She felt the heat of his touch and colour rushed to her cheeks.

'You've got paint on your face.'

He laughed. She tried to join him, but it didn't work for her. She turned towards the stairs, the paint brush still in her hand.

'Hey,' he called, 'leave your brush. I'll soak them overnight.'

She handed it to him across the distance, afraid to make contact, and forced herself to murmur, 'I'll make a cup of tea,' before she took off down the stairs.

Lance watched her, her fair hair, tamed beneath a scarf, bouncing across her shoulders, her trim little figure belying her age. What I need, he thought, is a good, stiff whisky. As he came down the stairs he could hear the kettle whistling. He wasn't going to take any more risks with Penny. His feelings for her were already running way beyond safety limits. When the boy arrived maybe he could start coming around again. Until then, if Andy wanted her checked out any further, he'd have to do it. As far as he was concerned there was nothing about Penny to find out anyway. Tomorrow he would tell Andy he was pulling out, spend a few days knocking over his paperwork before returning to the farm.

Penny's suspicions about his attention were growing. It had been pretty hairy back there when she challenged him about being on the Bluff this morning. Perhaps he was getting careless. Not a good sign. He'd better warn Andy to tread carefully. He put his head around the door.

'I'll give the tea a miss thanks, Penny.'

He yawned, started to stretch, realised he was about to hit his head, and dodged. Perhaps he should have let it happen. It might either have knocked some sense into him, or dulled his feelings.

'I'm ready to hit the sack.'

'Will you call again soon?'

Was that a note of disappointment in her voice? Forget it. Keep walking, mate. There's only one way to go, and that's out of her life.

'I don't know. I've got a pretty busy working schedule this coming week. You can ring the agency if you need anything. I'll say good-night, Penny.'

Abruptly, he turned into the hall leading to the front entrance.

'Lance,' she said, 'you've forgotten your sweater and anorak.'

That's the state she had him in! When he turned back to retrieve it, he noticed she still had a slight paint stain on her cheek. He longed to kiss her.

Keep going, Lance, old son. You're headed in the right direction. He plucked the jumper and coat from her arm.

'Have I done something to upset you?' she asked.

'Nah, I'm just tired.'

'I feel awful. I shouldn't have let you work so hard. Thanks for being so helpful. I don't understand why, but I'm grateful.'

'I think you do understand why,' he growled.

And without pausing to put on his sweater or coat, he wrenched open the door and stepped out into the night air. The southerly buffeted angrily against him as he made for his car. But it wasn't nearly as angry as he was with himself. He'd declared himself to Penny, and he had no right to. The sooner he could tell her the truth, the sooner he could walk away from all this with a clear conscience.

6

All night, Lance's words, 'I think you do understand why,' kept coming back to Penny. Tonight, the spark between them had been fanned into a flame and, she thought uneasily, would become an out-of-control fire, if she didn't slow things down. Settle in first, gradually introduce him to Jamie, give yourself time to know him better. You thought you would love Brad for ever when you married him. And then you found out how different you were.

Penny found sleep impossible. Lance crowded her thoughts. She wrapped herself in her doona, went out to the kitchen, stoked the fire, and curled up on the sofa with a book. Eventually it fell to the floor and she slept.

On Monday, the carpenter came to replace the window in the attic. Afterwards, to keep her mind occupied,

Penny unpacked Jamie's bed linen and made up his bed downstairs. Later, she called into the estate agency to sign the lease. Greg McCann greeted her, saying the documents would take a few days to prepare.

'What's the hold-up?' she asked anxiously.

'Andy Smith's out of town for a while, but you've got nothing to worry about. He's assured me the place is yours for as long as you want it.'

'Then I insist on paying a month's rent in advance, and I'd like to settle for the door locks and the other inconveniences.'

McCann gave her a receipt for the rent.

'You'll have to see Mr Patrick about the other things. It was his time and his money.'

Penny tried not to feel affronted. She didn't want to be obligated to Lance at this stage, but he was the type of man who'd laugh and say, 'It was nothing. You keep the melting moments and the soup coming and I'll do the rest.' Which wasn't good enough.

'I suppose he organised the mobile phone out of his pocket, too?'

'I don't know anything about that, Mrs Lawson.'

'Mr Patrick insisted I have one,' she explained, 'because he said it was going to take a while to get a line through.'

'I thought the cottage was already wired. I must have been mistaken. You'll have to take it up with Patrick. By the way, he left a parcel for you.'

Penny's heart lightened. As much as she hated to admit it, she'd been hoping to see Lance. The parcel meant at least he'd been thinking about her. It was wrapped in brown paper. She gave it a gentle rattle as she placed it in her shopping basket, denying her curiosity. She would open it in the privacy of her home.

When she finally did, she gasped with delight. It was a model aeroplane kit, accompanied by a note.

A small welcoming gift for Jamie.

When you're settled I'd be happy to come over and help him put it together and hang it from the attic ceiling. Thanks for dinner Sunday night.

Penny picked up the phone to thank him, then decided against it. She'd begun to take his presence, his help, for granted, and hadn't she resolved to slow things down? If she spoke to him she'd be tempted to ask him over for dinner again. Better to write a thank-you note. When Jamie arrived they could do it together.

That night, unable to relax, she pushed herself to finish painting the attic. It was after midnight when she surveyed it, and shrugged. Not the most professional job, and the floor and furniture needed polishing. It was as unlike her small son's bedroom at South Yarra as it could be, but the different feel, not the expense, was what mattered. She hoped Jamie would like it. She'd whipped up his enthusiasm for his very own attic bedroom during their daily phone conversations.

On Tuesday, when she arrived at her mother-in-law's apartment, Jamie threw himself into her arms. Her heart reached out to him, she held him close and tried not to cry.

'Mummy, are I going back with you to my new bedroom?' he asked.

'Am I, not are I, Bradley,' Alice Lawson corrected sternly.

Penny glared at the older woman. Jamie had been given Bradley James as his names, but was always called Jamie to avoid confusion with his father. The sooner he left with Penny the better.

'Yes, darling. We're going to have a quick lunch with Granny and then we're off on our big adventure.'

As they approached the cottage in the late afternoon, the wind seemed to whistle through even the tiniest openings in the car, to buffet it frighteningly. Jamie moved closer to her. She touched his little hand. It felt cold.

'It's OK, darling. We'll soon be inside in the warmth. Wait until you see the wonderful kitchen. It has this big, old stove.'

Parking the car as close as possible to the fence, Penny jumped out and reached across to lift her son out. Folding him tightly in her arms, shielding him, she ran to the front door, managed to open it without putting Jamie down, and surged inside, slamming it with her foot. She set him down in the passage, anxious at his wide eyes, his tight little mouth.

'Is we really going to live here?'

His voice trembled.

'Yes, darling. Isn't it a big adventure?'

'Like that story about that bad pirate?' he lisped.

She kissed his cheek.

'Yes, Jamie. Won't that be fun?'

His little face brightened.

'I guess.'

Then he spotted the stairs.

'Is that my cave up there?'

'Yes, but you can't sleep in it yet. It smells of paint. I've set up the room next to mine for the time being.'

'But, Mummy, I want to look.'

She nodded.

'All right, but don't run.'

She watched his thin, little legs as they carefully took each step, and vowed that he would grow strong, breathe easily at Bluff Cottage.

The days drifted by. Penny enrolled Jamie in kindergarten, checked him in with the local doctor, and they shopped. All the while, she hoped Lance would call, or that she might run into him. It puzzled and annoyed her at the one time, that she found herself looking for him at every turn of the street, in every shop. Every phone call had her racing to answer it.

Why hadn't he got back to her about the swimming lessons, about the model aeroplane, about the mobile phone? He had countless reasons to be in touch. She could, of course, have called into his office. In fact she did, supposedly to sign the lease, but when she asked, McCann told her, 'I'm sorry, Mr Patrick isn't available.'

That could mean many of several things, including, 'I don't want to see the widow if she calls.' Penny tried not to believe that, mainly because she didn't want to, but also because she knew he cared for her. He'd said as much.

At night, once Jamie was tucked into bed, she'd sit by the stove and ask herself the question over and over. Why didn't Lance get in touch?

Did it have something to do with the cottage itself, or could she indulge in the belief that he didn't trust himself alone with her? This made no sense now that Jamie was here. Perhaps it was the fact that she had a child and he wasn't into other people's children. More likely, she thought, disappointment flooding through her, he's met a glamorous woman. She'd never believed that empty diary routine he'd given her anyway.

She had to decide whether to ring him at his motel and make an arrangement for him to come to dinner, or forget the man with the impatient blue eyes. And she couldn't, not yet.

Spring arrived with a whimper. Occasionally the sun shone and the wind abated. She and Jamie found her cave together. They tidied it, brought away the rubbish in a garbage bag, made up stories about hidden treasure. Down on the shoreline, they left footprints in the damp sand, gathered shells, idled among the rocky pools looking for small sea urchins. Often they stopped to talk to a lone fisherman about this catch, and on one or two occasions, Penny had an odd feeling that they were being watched.

Jamie's health improved. He rarely needed his inhaler. But he kept asking when the man was coming to help him build his plane. Soon, she told him over and over, as keen as her little boy to believe that Lance was coming.

Penny decided against moving Jamie into the attic, for she now realised it was just too far from her at night. Instead it became a pirate's cave and they strung netting from the eaves, found an old suitcase in a second-hand shop, and turned it into a pirate's treasure chest, filling it with sea shells and cheap jewellery and vases from the charity shop. They played hide and seek and read exciting stories.

But Jamie missed his friends. Soon Penny would have the house and garden in a condition which enabled her to invite other children to stay overnight, and friends to spend the weekend, which set her thinking she'd been far too ambitious in believing she could do it all herself. Perhaps Lance's help and enthusiasm had made the impossible seem possible.

The move to Bluff Cottage was not quite working. If she hadn't met Lance . . . if she hadn't had his help, his presence . . . Nonsense, the sea air had made her lazy. She'd lost her edge, that was all. Saturday would be the day, she declared. Time to get someone in to help with the garden . . .

Lance sat in his motel room. Andy

had asked him to get all the paperwork in order before he baled out. This was his last week. After Sunday, his colleague had agreed to rule Penny out of the inquiry. The whole thing looked like a failure, anyway. His instincts didn't usually let him down, but for sure, if something was going to happen, it had to be in the next forty-eight hours.

During the intervening days, he'd half-hoped Penny would get in touch with him about the mobile phone or the swimming lessons, or something. Heaven knows, he'd given her ample excuses. But, he shrugged, why would she want him around now that she had her small son with her? Willpower he had plenty of, or so he thought, until tested by constant thoughts of her. He even dreamed about her falling down a cliff one night, and next morning was on the road, driving out to the Bluff to be sure she was OK, before he saw reason and swung the car around.

It was Friday evening. The brief spell of sunshine had given way to rain, which pounded on the motel's iron roof. He switched off the television, sighed, glared at the last of the reports to be finalised before he signed off on Sunday. First stop after that, the farm. There he'd work off his hang-up over the widow at Bluff Cottage.

After turning on the lap top, he sorted through an untouched file. A small piece of notepaper fell to the floor. It was grubby, folded into four. It wasn't one of his notes, probably a receipt for something. His training didn't permit him to throw anything away unread. He unfolded it.

Dear Lady Penelope, it began. It was enough to make him groan, to read on with a reluctant heart. *Thanks, foxy lady. We'll be down when it's all over*, it said.

Lance flopped on to the bed, his stomach in a knot. He wrenched off his boot, and threw it across to the other side of the room.

'When it's all over,' he repeated aloud.

What an ironic turn of phrase. So, it wasn't all over for him, not all over for the woman he had come to trust, to admire, to — he tried to fend off the word, but it would not be denied — love.

Come on, you're tough. You know the drill. Nobody falls in love with someone because they're small, alone, gutsy, and who has eyes the colour of melted chocolate.

'Especially not a cynical cop,' he added aloud to etch it into his brain. 'You are not going to compromise everything you've stood for in your career for a pair of dark eyes.'

He sat up, flattened out the note, re-read it, before retrieving his boot. Then he rustled through files and finally produced the sample of a known criminal's handwriting. He was no expert, but even a drover's dog could pick it. It matched that on the letter. His stomach now in a double knot, he forced himself to admit that Andy had to be told about this.

What really needled him was the fact that he'd been so easily hoodwinked by the widow. He should have gone with his instinct when she came into the agency. But no, macho man Patrick had allowed himself to get sucked in by the little lady. What a joke. Andy would think so anyway. He glanced at his watch. Too late to make the call tonight. Heaving his shoulders, he pushed on with his reports, trying to put what lay ahead of him out of his mind.

* * *

The rain eased to a gentle, reassuring sound as it fell on the iron roof over the kitchen. Penny stretched in her chair, her book fell from her lap as she listened, enjoying the sound, happy that the iron roof hadn't been replaced with slate tiles to match the front of the cottage. Next week, Sue and her husband, Geoff, were coming down. Geoff had agreed to help reorganise her furniture, and shift in her small antique purchases. The house looked lived in, cosy, and after last weekend's effort, the garden was starting to take shape.

Time she went to bed. She stood up, stretched, and then froze. What was that? Jamie? She picked up the torch which she always kept handy, and on tip-toe, hurried to his room. Smiling, she went to the side of the bed. He slept soundly. Her anxious breathing eased, she placed her lips to his brow, readjusted the quilt over him, and crept from the room. Perhaps he'd called out in his sleep. She was on her way into her bedroom, when she heard the noise again. This time she identified it as a scuffling sound and thought it came from the attic.

A rat! Please, don't let it be a rat. She had no idea what to do if it were, but she returned to the kitchen and grabbed the poker. At every step she took on her way up the stairs, she expected a creaking sound, and then realised with a wry smile that if it were a rat, it would scamper. And tonight that wouldn't be a bad outcome. She could deal with it tomorrow.

She promised herself, as she got closer to the attic door, that as independent as she wanted to be, she needed a good friend down here. Someone like Lance, who could advise her. If a rat was scurrying around the attic, she wouldn't be able to set foot in it until it was flushed out. That necessitated a pest controller coming down from the nearest big city, miles away. In the meantime . . . well, even with the door closed, she wouldn't be able to sleep at night, knowing it, and its family were running wild.

Her mind ran wild, too. She tried to talk the rat theory down. It was more likely to be a branch slapping against the window pane. Well, go in, she told herself as she paused at the door, her heart pounding.

'Is anyone there?' she said, her voice dropping to almost inaudible with each word. She'd always thought it a foolish question when she'd heard it asked on films, for if anyone was actually hiding, they wouldn't answer. But she asked it anyway.

She started to tremble in the silence, and clutched the poker more firmly. With her shoulder, she gently edged the door wider. The curtains were never pulled in the attic, and at night she left the window ajar by an inch or two. Now it stood wide open. Drops of rain glistened on its ledge. An eerie apology for moonlight shone into the room. A frisson of fear raced through her as she moved her torch across the room. It caught the shadowed figure of a person slumped on the floor to one side of the window. She heard a whimpering sound. Breathing quickly, Penny kept her torch beam on the figure. Her fear turned to anxiety.

'Who is it? What's the matter?'

The light picked up the visitor's eyes. They were the eyes of a woman, a woman who looked — afraid wasn't quite the word. More likely upset that she'd been caught. A surfie looking for shelter from the rain?

'Don't move,' Penny demanded, brandishing the poker. 'What's your name?'

The woman shivered noticeably in the torchlight.

'I've hurt my . . . my ankle,' she whispered.

Penny moved closer. Suddenly the woman stuck her foot out, and Penny stumbled over it. As she fell, the torch and poker dropped from her hand. Quickly her assailant was on her feet, shining the torch in her eyes. Temporarily blinded, Penny heard her name fall from the lips of her unwelcome visitor.

'Penny,' the voice said again, this time whispered in an appealing tone. 'Surely it can't be dear old Lady Penelope?'

Penny stood up and pushed the torch aside.

'Yes, I'm Penny. Who are you?' she demanded.

'Don't you recognise me?'

Penny needed breathing space, time

to collect her thoughts. Although the woman didn't seem to pose any danger, she could be pretending she knew her. She had already tricked her once.

'Let me turn on the light,' she said, flicking on the switch, and then turning to face her visitor.

She drew in her breath. Could it be? The woman looked awful, thin, haggard, her damp hair hanging limply to her shoulders. She shivered under Penny's gaze.

'Shelley, is that you, Shelley?'

'Yes, it's me,' her visitor whispered, and flung herself into Penny's arms.

7

Penny hugged her dishevelled friend. She had so many questions to ask, but they could wait. Shelley obviously needed help.

'Shelley, you look awful. You're shivering, and you're soaked. Come downstairs, where it's warm. I've got the old combustion stove going.'

'It sounds like heaven.'

Shelley's voice shook. She leaned heavily against Penny as they made their way down to the kitchen. There, Penny helped her off with her wet duffel coat, and outer garments and offered her her dressing-gown. Then she drew up a chair for her by the stove, and towelled her hair dry.

'That's better. Are you warming up?'

Shelley nodded as she huddled by the fire. Curbing her curiosity a little longer, Penny made a pot of tea, and settled beside Shelley on a chair.

'Now, Shelley, tell me all about it. What on earth were you doing up there in the attic?'

Shelley sipped her tea, as if putting off her answer. Penny didn't hurry her. Shelley finally looked up.

'If I'd known you were here, I'd have knocked on the door. But I thought maybe squatters or undesirables had settled in, and I didn't want to risk it. Gosh, I'm hungry, Penny. Can I have something to eat?'

'Would a toasted sandwich be all right?'

Shelley nodded.

'Thanks. So how come you're staying here?'

'I'm renting the cottage, but have plans to buy the place. Can you believe that? After all these years, I had a yearning to visit, and when I saw the cottage was for sale, well, I couldn't resist it. It was always my fantasy to own it. Always the place I loved best when I was growing up.'

Penny prepared the sandwich as she spoke, vaguely uneasy that she was the person answering the questions, when it was Shelley who had the explaining to do.

'You were such a romantic, little kid. I see you still haven't moved into the real world. How could you want to live down here?'

Shelley laughed harshly.

'All that pirate stuff and shipwrecked lover! Good heavens! I cringe when I think about it.'

'But we had such fun. Surely you remember.'

'I remember all those silly games we used to play in the caves and burying a bottle or something. Sometimes . . .'

She stopped there, as if she'd decided not to say the rest.

'How's that sandwich coming?'

'It's on the way.'

Upset by Shelley's remarks, Penny began to wonder if this was the same person she'd loved and shared so much with in her youth. Handing her the sandwich on a plate, she spoke firmly.

'I don't think you told me what you were doing up in the attic. I'd like to know, Shelley.'

Shelley tackled the sandwich as if she were very hungry. Penny waited for her to finish eating.

'It's a long story. I came down here, thinking the old place would be empty, and I could stay for a while. You see, I've been sick. I picked up some bug overseas some time ago, and every now and then it makes me very ill. It means I can't work regularly, and money gets pretty tight.'

'I'm sorry,' Penny said, and waited for her to go on. 'So how on earth did you get into the attic?'

Shelley put the plate aside.

'Through the window, of course. Conveniently I found a ladder propped against the veranda post. I climbed up and from the veranda it was easy to get on to the house roof and then to the attic window.'

'I'd forgotten I left the ladder out. We

were trimming back the climbing roses. When you saw the light, why didn't you go back to town to a motel?'

Shelley yawned. She looked dishevelled, worn out, with dark smudges under her lifeless eyes. It shocked Penny that her once pretty friend looked so ill. Penny had envied her, her dark wavy hair, her china blue eyes, the attention she always received from people.

'I'm short of money. Besides, I wasn't thinking too clearly, Lady Penelope. The bug does that to me. Could I stay tonight, and we can talk again in the morning?'

Penny didn't have the heart to press her for more information.

'Of course you can. The bunk's made up in the attic, if you can fight your way through the fish netting and junk. My little boy plays up there.'

'I'm so tired, if there's a bed behind it, I could fight my way through anything.'

Shelley didn't comment on her

135

having a child, which disappointed Penny. She excused it on her friend's illness. The quicker she got her to bed, the quicker she'd recover and be able to fill in the details.

'You can take up a couple of hot water bottles. You might like to have a shower first to warm up.'

'I'm too out of it to shower, but I'll have those hot water bottles.'

Penny took empty bottles from a hook on the back door and filled them from the kettle.

'Do you need any help up the stairs?'

'I'll manage. Thanks, Pen.'

Shelley's attempted smile didn't quite succeed. Penny waited for her to reach the top of the stairs, before she checked on Jamie and then retired herself. But sleep evaded her. For hours she worried about her old friend. What had befallen Shelley over the years? She was no longer the vibrant, energetic person she had once been. She'd hardened, developed a sharpness, was at times almost rude. The chronic illness was obviously to blame. In the morning she'd press her friend for the full story, and hopefully work out a way to help her towards recovery.

It was well into the next day, and Shelley had not appeared. Penny decided to take her a breakfast tray and invited Jamie to join her to meet their guest. The attic door lay closed. Tapping on it, Penny pushed it open, as they waited for Shelley's response.

Shelley swung around. She looked flustered, was already dressed, and searching through the big wardrobe.

'Oh, it's you, Penny,' she said, and then glancing at Jamie, added, 'And who is this?'

'My son, Jamie. Say hello to Aunty Shelley, Jamie. You remember I told you all about her.'

'Hello. You is sleeping in my cave,' he said.

'So it's your cave now? Did you know it used to be mine? I'm taking it over for a while. OK kid?' Shelley said.

Penny gazed at Shelley and felt her

heart quicken. She wasn't at all sure she wanted this new Shelley to stay on.

'How long were you planning to stay? Earlier, you said overnight,' Penny asked, uncertain.

'Not long. A day or two, if you'll have me. I promise I won't be any trouble. I'll spend most of the day resting in the attic.'

She turned such doleful eyes on Penny, how could she refuse?

'Well, Jamie,' Penny said and turned to her son, 'you wouldn't mind if Aunty Shelley took over the cave for a bit, would you?'

'Don't ask him to call me aunty. I hate that kind of thing. Call me Shelley, kid. So what do you say? Do I get to be boss of the cave for a while?'

Jamie turned his eyes up to his mother.

'Is she a bad pirate, Mummy?'

'That's me, a bad pirate, out to steal your treasure.'

'You can't have it then,' Jamie shrilled.

'I'm joking, kid,' Shelley said abrasively. 'So that's settled. Thanks for the breakfast, by the way. I'll bring the tray down when I'm finished.'

Penny felt she'd been dismissed in her own home, and she didn't like it, but in front of Jamie she couldn't say anything.

'See you soon,' she said, taking Jamie's hand and leaving.

Perhaps Shelley still thought of it as her cottage, Penny rationalised. But try as she did, she couldn't come to terms with Shelley's changed personality. Her friend had always been high-spirited, game, but never ill-mannered or abrasive. Again Penny excused it on her illness. The sooner Shelley felt better, the sooner she'd leave, and as much as Penny disliked thinking it, she now admitted she didn't want her visitor here for too long. The new Shelley set a bad example for Jamie, and didn't fit into her plans for life at the Bluff.

As Penny put a batch of scones into the oven, she heard a knock at the door.

Jamie could just reach the knob, and in a sing-song voice, said, 'I'll open the door,' as he skipped along the passage.

She followed him and heard a voice, a familiar voice say, 'Let me guess. You're young Jamie.'

Her son giggled.

'How does you know me?'

'I'm a friend of your mother's, and she told me all about you. Is she in?'

Penny wanted to feel unmoved, nonchalant, at the sound of Lance's voice, but she couldn't help the beat of her heart, the colour which flamed in her cheeks. She almost cried out his name as she flung off her apron in a cloud of flour. Lance, she said under her breath, and then she paused, gripped the side of the door and urged herself to settle down, slow down.

As she stepped into the hallway, she saw him and her little boy, holding hands, coming towards her. He looked so strong, so masculine, and maybe because he looked so comfortable holding Jamie's hand, the aura of loneliness which sometimes surrounded him had disappeared.

'He's your friend, Mummy,' Jamie said, beaming.

'He's a fair-weather friend. I don't think he likes my soup.'

Penny smiled and turned to Lance, hoping he'd share her joke, but instead found only shadows in his eyes. The joy at seeing him blurred.

'Have you come to help Jamie with his model aeroplane?' she asked.

Lance sniffed the air.

'Sure, and to help you eat whatever it is you've got in the oven.'

He turned to the boy.

'What do you say, little guy? Do we eat first, or work on the aeroplane?'

Jamie jumped up and down.

'I get my plane.'

He went racing upstairs, almost colliding with Shelley on her way down.

'Good morning,' she said, focusing on Lance. 'I didn't know we had a visitor, Penny. Aren't you going to introduce me?'

Penny felt ambushed, wishing she'd had time to mention Shelley to Lance before her friend, who looked marginally better, appeared.

'Lance, I'd like you to meet Shelley. You remember I mentioned her? This used to be her parents' cottage.'

He stepped forward, offered his hand.

'Lance Patrick,' he said. 'What brings you back to these parts?'

'I've been ill, and Penny suggested I recuperate here.'

Penny stared at Shelley. She couldn't remember suggesting any such thing, but loyalty kept her silent.

'I noticed a car broken down along the road. I got worried. Thought I'd call in and see if everything was OK out here,' Lance said. 'Is it yours, Shelley?'

Penny hurried into the kitchen.

'Excuse me. I'd better get the scones from the oven,' she said, one ear on the conversation.

'Yes, and I need my suitcase,' Shelley was saying. 'I don't suppose you could run me out to collect it and maybe have a look at the car, Mr Patrick? I think I've run out of petrol.'

'Call me Lance, and I'd be glad to, but I've promised the little bloke I'll help him put his plane together. If you can wait until after then . . . '

He raised his broad shoulders.

'But I need a change of clothes before I shower. It won't take us long.'

Shelley looked down at her crumpled shirt and jeans and then over to Jamie.

'You don't mind waiting do you, kid?'

'I'll take you out, Shelley.'

Penny wrapped the hot scones in a towel, noting the disappointment on Jamie's face.

'But you don't know anything about cars.'

'I always keep a spare can of petrol here. If the problem is something else, we can ring the local garage and get them to come out and look at it.'

'Come on, Mr Lance,' Jamie said, taking Lance's hand. 'I get my plane from the cave.'

That settled it.

Shelley's now dry duffel coat hung on a peg by the door. Penny took it down and handed it to her.

'It'll give us a chance to talk,' she said. 'Have you got your car keys?' she asked, pulling on her parka.

In Penny's car, Shelley smiled at her.

'You sly, little fox. Where did you get that handsome devil?'

Penny raised her brows.

'I didn't get him. I met him when I called into the real estate agency about the cottage. He's been very helpful, and a good friend. Now, I'm dying to hear your story. What's been happening to you? What happened last night?'

'What's to tell? You know it all. I felt so lousy. I threw a few things in the car and came down here on impulse, expecting the cottage to be vacant. My car stalled on the road. I walked to the cottage in the rain, and when I saw the lights on in the house, the ladder, it seemed I was meant to crawl into the attic, get some sleep, and . . . well . . . at that stage I couldn't think beyond there.'

'So what have you been doing with yourself all these years, Shelley? Why did you stop writing? I missed you.'

'When you're back-packing around the world, letter writing isn't your first priority. Tell me about you. Married, obviously, and divorced?'

Penny briefly detailed Brad's death, her feeling that she'd been spared to start a new life, and her move to Sandy Bluff.

'The old place was in a pretty bad condition. You should have been there when we cleaned out the attic. Gosh, we threw out some junk, but you'll be interested in something I found.'

'Not a treasure map?' Shelley mocked.

'More interesting than that. Your old Bruno bear. You gave him such a hard time, the poor old thing only had one eye.'

'Old Bruno? I wondered where he'd got to.'

Shelley sounded alive for the first time.

'I hope you didn't throw him out. I'd like to have him.'

'No, I didn't throw him out,' Penny replied.

She had a crisis of conscience. She'd tossed Bruno into the washing machine and he'd fallen apart. She'd forgotten old teddy bears weren't made of washable material. After Shelley recovered her good humour would be soon enough to tell her Bruno was no more. Fortunately, they'd reached Shelley's car and the bear was forgotten.

It took only minutes to pour the petrol into the empty tank and with a sense of relief, Penny heard the engine roar into life. She hoped it meant Shelley wouldn't stay long, and hated herself for feeling that way. Shelley said she had something to do in town, and would be back later. Penny told her not to hurry, and then drove slowly back to the house to enable Lance and Jamie to have time together.

They were sitting at the kitchen table when she returned, the fragile little plane now firmly glued together. As she entered, Jamie beamed at her.

'Look, Mummy,' he said excitedly, picking up the aircraft.

Holding it, he zoomed it up and down, making an engine noise with his little rosy cheeks puffed out. Penny turned a wide smile in Lance's direction.

'It's wonderful, sweetheart. Did you say thank you to Mr Lance?'

'Thank you, Mr Lance.'

He raced out of the kitchen door and into the hallway, still zooming away with his arms and mouth.

Penny buttered the scones while Lance made a pot of tea. She didn't even wonder at how comfortable and natural it seemed. As he stretched his long legs, his mug of tea in one hand, he turned to her.

'So Shelley's gone to town? Will she be back soon?'

'She didn't say,' Penny replied.

'How well do you know her?'

'I used to know her very well. Now, I'm not so sure. She's changed.'

'In what way?' Lance asked.

'It's her illness, I suppose. She used to be so pretty, but now she's sort of hard.'

'What's wrong with her?'

'I don't know exactly, but she picked up some bug while she was overseas, and every now and again it manifests itself. I hear they're very resistant. Anyway, she arrived here last night, hoping to find the cottage empty, and when she saw lights she climbed up into the attic. That's where I found her.'

'In the attic? Odd, isn't it? So you didn't invite her here?'

'I haven't heard from her in years. I had trouble recognising her. You're very interested in her, Lance.'

'I'm a bit suspicious of people who wander around the Bluff in the middle of the night. Why the devil didn't she knock on the door? Don't you find that a bit odd, Penny?'

'She didn't know I was living here, but I admit I did think it strange.'

He took another scone from the plate.

'These are real good. Maybe you'll teach me how to whip up a batch of real scones one day.'

His grin brightened the gloom which had settled over them.

'Any time.'

She brushed her mouth with her index finger in case it had gathered a coating of flour or crumbs.

'Penny, are you sure she is Shelley? Could she be someone who looks like your old friend?'

Penny shook her head.

'No. She's changed, but not that much. Besides, we've talked. She remembers all the antics we used to get up to.'

Jamie came zooming back into the room.

'Can you hang the plane in the cave, Mr Lance?' he asked.

'Sure can, little mate. Let's ask

Mummy if its OK to go into Shelley's room first.'

'I'm sure she won't mind. You'll need some string.'

Penny found some in the kitchen drawer and they went upstairs, hand in hand, chatting like old friends. It was so good for Jamie to have a male influence around the place. Penny hugged herself as she cleared the dishes and began preparing lunch.

They were still upstairs when Shelley came in. She looked less tense, clearer eyed.

Throwing her coat over a chair, she said, 'I notice the king pirate's car outside. I take it he's still here.'

Penny laughed.

'I've invited him for lunch.'

'I wouldn't let him go home ever again if he belonged to me.'

'Shelley, he doesn't belong to me. We're friends, no more.'

'The way you flash those eyes at him? Come on, Pen, stop playing make believe and grab him. He'll get away if you don't. The good-looking ones always do.'

Shelley flopped into a chair.

'By the way, you mentioned finding my old bear. Where is poor Bruno?'

Penny nearly dropped the plate she was holding. She should have had a ready answer, but hadn't expected Shelley to even care. After all, she'd left the bear behind when she moved to town years ago.

'Um . . . Bruno . . . well.'

She hesitated, reluctant to tell Shelley its fate.

'Yes, Bruno,' Shelley repeated.

'I wanted to keep it for old times' sake, but it was so stained and dusty.'

'And?'

Shelley stood up, her voice on the rise.

'I threw it into the washing machine and it sort of . . . sort of disintegrated.'

'You what?'

Shelley's face glowed red.

'How dare you!'

She advanced menacingly towards

Penny. For a minute Penny thought she might strike her, but she dropped on to the old sofa, as if her legs wouldn't carry her any farther.

'I didn't think it was that important to you. I'm sorry. I'll buy you another one. I know it won't be the same, but . . .'

'Won't be the same? You have no idea what you're saying, you stupid woman.'

'I beg your pardon? I won't listen to that kind of talk in my home.'

Suddenly Shelley put her head in her hands and began to weep.

'What happened to the bits of the bear? What did you do with them?' she mumbled.

'I threw them in the bin. There was nothing left but straw and one eye. I'm sorry I didn't know you cared so much about him.'

Shelley leaped from the sofa.

'But there had to be more. What did you do with the remnants? Did you sort through them?'

She shook Penny with a strength she

didn't think Shelley had.

'What did you do with the bits and pieces? Don't lie to me. I know there was more,' she screamed.

8

Lance arrived in the kitchen as Penny pushed Shelley away. The woman's knees buckled under her and she fell to the floor.

'What the devil's going on here? Why all the shouting?'

He raced to Penny's side. She was shaking, had her hands to her head.

'Dear heaven, what have I done?' she was murmuring.

He lifted Shelley from the floor and placed her on the sofa. He put two fingers to the pulse in her neck, breathed easier. She was all right. Straightening up, he put a protective arm around Penny.

'Don't worry. You haven't done anything. Your friend's breathing is OK. She's probably fainted. What happened here?'

Penny looked at him with clouded eyes.

'I don't quite know. It was over the teddy bear. It fell apart in the washing machine. When I told Shelley, she grabbed me, shouted at me. I pushed her away and she crumpled at my feet. I didn't strike her, Lance.'

'Of course you didn't. I saw what happened. You couldn't hurt a fly.'

His arm tightened about her to offer her reassurance.

'She's not thinking straight. That's all.'

'I think we should call a doctor, in case she's having a recurrence of her illness. Where's Jamie? I don't want him down here until we sort this out.'

Her chin quivered, as if she were about to cry.

'He's fine. I told him to hide in the cave until I yelled that the pirate ship had disappeared. I'll see if I can revive Shelley.'

He spoke gently to the woman's limp form, calling her name, once twice, but without response. Looking back at Penny, he said, 'I won't muck around here. I'll get her to the hospital.'

What he couldn't tell Penny was that he believed the woman was desperate and would do anything to get what she wanted. His first priority was to get Shelley to hospital without alarming Penny. Later he would sit down quietly with her and explain things.

Penny stroked Shelley's brow.

'Poor thing. She was so pretty, so pretty, and now look at her. Surely there's something they can do to get rid of that bug.'

'We'll see. They can run some tests in hospital. I'll get Doc Kelly to admit her for a day or two. See what can be done. After that, well, let's talk about it later. Now, go get Jamie and do some exploring together. But don't bring back any pirates. This place is crowded enough at the moment,' he said, trying to bring some light back into her gentle eyes.

She came to his side and touched his arm. He gazed down at her as she stretched up and kissed his cheek.

'I've started to think of you as my genie. You always turn up when I need help. Do you have a sixth sense, or what? How can I thank you?'

He'd have settled for another kiss, a chance to hold her and run his hands through her hair. But as usual he had to settle for something a lot less satisfying, and gave her the kind of answer she probably expected.

'While you keep the home cooking guaranteed, I'll keep coming around.'

Shelley stirred.

'Off you go,' he said. 'Better if you're not here when she wakes. Perhaps you don't realise it, but she's a taker, and she's working on your generosity.'

'I know, but I want to help her, Lance. She's short of money, and she used to be a very good friend.'

'But you don't owe her. Before we go making any decisions, let's see what the doctor has to say.'

He was anxious to get the woman away from the house. He couldn't be sure, or say anything to Penny, but

Lance was convinced she was on drugs. If she were, to feed her habit, she would manipulate anyone, even her best friend, with the desperation of an addict. He'd seen it played out before. Grabbing coats from kitchen pegs, he thrust them in Penny's direction.

'Tell Jamie you have to sneak out of the house to avoid waking the wicked pirate,' he said.

He waited, pacing, restless, until he heard them creep downstairs whispering quietly, cross the passage, and finally open the front door. Lance put his head around the kitchen entrance, saw the front door close quietly, and breathed more easily. Still, he waited until he judged Penny and her son to be well away from the house. Then he picked up the limp figure of Shelley Anderson, carried her to his car and drove her to Doc Kelly's surgery.

On the journey, his thoughts fought for a plan. He knew without question that Anderson, not Penny, was the woman he'd been waiting for, which filled him with hope. But it was too early to celebrate. He'd found his woman, but that was only step one, and if Anderson were a drug addict, it could complicate things, make her more daring, impulsive, less predictable. He couldn't afford to let her out of his sight until she made her next move.

Shelley came to in Doc Kelly's surgery, as he examined her eyes, and she immediately demanded to leave. She lacked the strength to fight off Lance's restraining arm, however, and finally, she admitted her drug habit. It had begun with her trying to ease the pain and debilitating affects of the bug, she said, and agreed to go to hospital for a few days for further tests, but only if she could return to Bluff Cottage to recuperate. Lance agreed readily and accompanied her in the ambulance to the hospital in the next town. Mean-time, by phone, he filled in Andy and arranged for him to keep someone posted outside her hospital room during her stay.

As he made his way back to Bluff Cottage, Lance cursed. He rehearsed over and over in his mind how he would tell Penny their friendship had been based on deception, that originally his help had been given to curry favour, to get inside her mind, to discover if she was the woman they were after. But somewhere along the way he had fallen in love with her dark eyes, her loving, thoughtful nature. No, he thought, better to leave that last bit out, at least until he got everything else out of the way. He had to ask her for a huge favour, something he had no right to ask, but ask it he would. His job, his commitment required it.

She and Jamie were in the garden picking roses when he pulled the car up by the picket fence. Jamie raced to his side.

'We frightened the bad pirate away. She's gone,' he cried. 'I never thinked of a lady pirate.'

Lance smiled through his anxiety, patting the child on the head.

'Shelley wasn't a bad pirate, little mate, she was sick, and now she's gone to get better. When she comes back, you'll see how nice she is.'

Penny looked sharply at Lance. So he'd arranged for Shelley to come back here. It would have been nice to be consulted.

'How is she?' she asked.

'Hospitalised for a few days for tests. Penny, when can we talk?'

She'd never see his eyes so dull, so troubled, his mouth so tight. It wasn't going to be good talk. Was he leaving town? Getting married? Her mind sorted through the possibilities. Yet she managed to answer brightly.

'Jamie's due for a nap, aren't you, darling?'

'If Mr Lance reads me a story first.'

'Sure, little mate. One story coming up.'

'I've kept you some lunch,' Penny said. 'Will you have it afterwards?'

He nodded.

Half-an-hour later, they sat across the table from one another. Lance took a drink from his mug then laid it on the table.

'This is about the most difficult thing I've ever had to do, Penny.'

Then don't do it, she wanted to cry out, but she waited, gripping her mug, avoiding his eyes.

'You've become the most important person in the world to me.'

Her heart leaped and then crashed. Why did he look so despondent?

'But our growing friendship is based on a lie. I'm not who you think I am. I'm not in real estate. I'm a farmer.'

'So you misled me a bit. I always knew there was something odd about your story. But, somehow I trusted you. I love farmers.'

He pushed on.

'That's just the beginning. You see, I used to be a detective. Recently I was persuaded to help the Force on a special job, to finish a task I started ten years ago.'

Penny felt her eyes widen.

'You're in the police?'

'Not officially. Let me go on. Ten years ago, a huge bank robbery took place in Melbourne. We nailed the two men, but didn't recover the money or arrest the person who drove the getaway car. Those two men are due to be released from prison this week. We expect them to make contact with the person who drove the car and stashed the money.'

'It's fascinating, but what's it to do with me, with us, with anyone at Sandy Point?'

He stood up, walked across to the stove and turned his back to it, the tip of his tongue moistening his lips.

'Word filtered back to the Force over the years that the money was hidden somewhere here, at Bluff Cottage. We've been over the place again and again. We set up a room here, lived in at various stages, but with no response.'

Penny was beginning to see things more clearly, slot together some of the jigsaw pieces which earlier she'd conveniently tried to dismiss.

'So you decided the money isn't hidden here? Why did you stay on?'

Even though he'd deceived her, she could forgive him. He was doing his duty and, if only he'd answer, 'Because I met you.'

'This is where it gets really tough. Believe me, Penny, after that first meeting with you it got tougher by the hour. I fell for your dark eyes, your gentleness, your love of homely things, in a big way. You weren't like any other woman I'd known.'

'There's a but about to come up, isn't there?' she broke in, a tightness developing in her throat. 'So say it. You're married, aren't you?'

He laughed harshly, shook his head.

'It's not that simple. When you came into the agency demanding to buy Bluff Cottage, you aroused my interest, my professional interest. I asked myself why you wanted that old dump so desperately, and there seemed to be only one answer. Can you guess the rest?'

She twisted the mug slowly in her

hand. Of course she could guess the rest! She wasn't stupid. But she would make him say it, make him burn.

'You tell me,' she said coldly.

'I didn't want to believe it, but look at it from my viewpoint. I was on the look-out for a woman, about thirty, who knew the area well, and wanted access to the cottage. You fitted the frame, except, you weren't at all like the woman I was expecting.'

Penny put down her mug, pushed a loose strand of hair from her face. A nervous giggle welled up inside her, but she kept it in check. She'd come down to Sandy Bluff to chase a dream, to change her dull, dependent life, and now Mr Detective Patrick was telling her she'd been a major player in a real-life drama.

'You thought I drove the getaway car and that I hid the money?'

He nodded.

'For a while. I told myself over and over it couldn't be you, but your fascination with caves, solitary strolls on the shore, the attic, your moneyed background. I asked myself why you'd want to buy Bluff Cottage when you had a city apartment. It didn't add up, until I knew more about you. I should have gone with my instinct. It told me from the start you were exactly what you said you were. But to be successful, cops develop suspicious natures, devious minds. You mightn't believe this, but I'd decided to call it quits and go back to the farm, but then I found that note.'

'What note?' Penny asked quickly.

'I found it tucked in amongst the rubbish we cleared out of the attic. It was addressed to Lady Penelope and said something like, 'We'll be down when it's all over.''

'To Lady Penelope? But I didn't get a note like that,' Penny uttered in amazement.

'Of course you didn't. I know that now. It's obvious your so-called best friend was using your nickname. Please, I'm asking you to be open-minded, to understand my dilemma. I never meant to hurt you.'

But he had badly wounded her sense of self, her pride, clean-bowled any chance she had of happiness with the man with the impatient blue eyes. She'd chased down her dream and found it had no substance.

Penny longed to go back to this morning, when she and Lance had shared that intimate moment after Shelley's collapse. She yearned to rewind the tape and record something different after that moment, but the realisation that you can't go on running away from real life had finally caught up with her. That's what she'd been doing down here — running away.

'Lance,' she said, 'what's done is done. We all make mistakes. Mine was to take you at face value when all along your actions seemed odd. I should have been questioning them. Shall we say goodbye now before Jamie wakes up?'

'The job's not finished, Penny. And it can't be unless you agree to help.'

He made a move towards her, but checked himself.

'We need your help. If it were for myself, I wouldn't ask, but it's at last within our scope to recover the money and close the case.'

She linked her fingers together, tried to stay calm, though her spine tingled, her heart raced.

'How can I possibly help?'

'The woman who has all the answers is your friend, Shelley Anderson. She drove the getaway car, she has the money hidden somewhere, and she'll go for it in the next few days. If we can catch her . . . '

Penny's eyes misted.

'Shelley? I can't believe it. And yet . . . '

'You must know she's not the same person she was as a girl. She's cunning, manipulative, and she thinks she can walk all over you. She's anxious to come back here to stay for a few days. She has to have a reason. There's something here she needs.

My plan is to . . . '

'I don't want to hear it,' Penny cried out. 'I've been blind about you, blind about Shelley, but now I know the truth, I can't possibly have her back. I have my son to consider. You can see that. Sorry, but you'll have to find another way to get your evidence. No way will I risk Jamie's well-being.'

'I understand. I hated asking, but for safety, I'm recommending that you take Jamie back to-stay with his grand-mother, for the time being anyway. He can't be around while Anderson's still free. Nothing's going to stop your friend from coming back. Whatever it is that's here will draw her back. If you're reluctant to help, I advise you to go, too.'

Rage welled up in Penny.

'How dare you do this to me? Play around with my life, endanger my little boy, ruin everything. Get out. I don't want to see you ever again.'

He caught her raised fists, restrained her, slipped his arms around her, held her. But only until she came to her senses and realised she shouldn't be there. He was her enemy. She struggled free.

'Goodbye, Lance,' she said, holding back the tears.

9

Penny lay awake most of the night, her mind on alert, the possibilities sending shivers along her spine. What if Shelley came back to the house in the middle of the night? She'd done it once before, climbed into the attic, obviously desperate to find whatever it was she'd hidden there. But what could it be?

What if the bank robbers, released from prison, planned to join her here? She should have asked Lance to come back. She shouldn't have brought her son to this lonely spot to live. It only worked so long as Lance was around. She switched on the bedside light and picked up the book she'd been reading, but the words flashed by meaninglessly.

Slamming it closed, she swung out of bed, and, poker in hand, checked the window in the attic, though she clearly remembered closing it earlier. Then she made sure the front and back doors were secure. Whatever happened in the next few days, Penny decided, she couldn't leave Jamie down here. Lance had been right to suggest he go back to stay with his grandmother until things settled down — until Shelley was apprehended.

A knife twisted in her heart. There was nothing she could do for her old friend. Lance had already persuaded her that kindness and compassion, the gifts she could offer Shelley, would be lost on the woman. She needed constant professional help. Perhaps Penny could assist later with the cost of that.

After examining the front door, a picture suddenly flashed before her. Something connected in her mind. Shelley's certainty, her angry insistence that there was more than straw and an eye left of Bruno bear pressed her memory buttons. She remembered for the first time that there was something else. She'd found it the next day. After preparing to do a load of washing, she'd found a small key in the bottom of the machine. That's what Shelley was after! That small, innocent-looking key!

Adrenalin pumped through her body as she waited for the sun to come up, for a respectable hour to ring Lance. As she waited she decided that the quickest way to get things cleared up was for her to co-operate with the investigation. In her heart she had known it from the moment of Lance's suggestion, but since she'd met the man with impatient blue eyes, her heart had sent her so many conflicting messages that it was no longer reliable. She had thought herself falling in love with him. But how could you love someone who had deceived you so badly, suspected you of criminal activities, used you? She groaned, called his name silently.

At eight, with Jamie's bag already packed, she rang Alice Lawson.

'Would you like a little guest for a few days?' she asked, trying to sound carefree. 'I want to paint the rest of the house.'

Next, she called Lance on his mobile.

'I'm taking Jamie back to his gran's today. I should be home around five. Can I see you then?'

'You're making the right decision for the little bloke. You should stay on with your ma-in-law, too. I'll let you know when we've cleared up the case.'

'I've changed my mind. I want to help. You can bring Shelley back to the cottage tomorrow. But first I want to talk to you.'

She decided to say no more.

'You're a real trooper, Penny. With you around, it's going to speed things up. Shelley trusts you. You'll be quite safe. We'll have people watching the place every second, and I'll be around. If I thought there was a chance you might be in danger . . .'

He choked on the rest of the sentence. It occurred to her then that he wasn't far away.

'Where are you?' she asked.

'I slept in the car down the track. I wanted to be sure you and the little guy were all right.'

'I bet you didn't sleep. Me neither.'

She hung up then, choking with tears of gratitude — and love?

The day turned hot, sultry. Penny felt drained after her return trip with Jamie. She wiped her forehead with a tissue, then placed her key in the cottage door. She opened it slowly, quelling a tremor of fear which threatened to overwhelm her. Fear of what? Once she had looked upon this scene with a dream in her heart. Now the dream cottage had turned into a place of silent menace.

Shaking herself, she went inside and glanced at her watch. Lance was due at any moment. Perhaps even now he was watching the cottage from a hidden spot. She had to hide her uneasiness and her nervousness from him, for she didn't want to be a passenger. She wanted to be a player from now on. Throwing off her jacket, she filled the kettle, made herself think of Lance's reaction when she told him about the key! Since early this morning she'd searched her memory for its location. She'd put it down carelessly. But where? Then she recalled what she'd had on that day — her jeans.

When the knock came to the door, she started, then stood silent. It had to be Lance. She straightened her shoulders and hurried to let him in. He came through the door with a confident stride, but there was no mistaking his artificial smile. How she longed to see his blue eyes gleam, his face light up with a reassuring grin, but too much had passed between them. They had moved on.

'A cup of tea?' she asked.

'I'll go for that.'

He sounded as uncomfortably cheerful as she felt.

He took the mug from her and eased his tall frame on to the sofa.

'Look, Penny, you don't have to do this. Shelley will come back to the place anyway. We can keep her under surveillance. We'll nab her after she's found whatever it is.'

'I know what it is, Lance.'

He shifted to face her.

'Yeah?'

She sank her hand into the old jeans she'd changed into, withdrawing the small key.

'This,' she said holding it aloft.

'You little beauty. That's it.'

He leaped to his feet, took the key from her, caught her in his arms and waltzed her around the room.

'You little beauty. Meeting you is the best thing that's ever happened to me, Lady Penelope.'

Breathless, she smiled.

'I take it that means you're pleased with me.'

'Pleased?'

He stopped, lifted her chin with his finger.

'You know what this means?'

The gleam had returned to his eyes as she nodded.

'I think I do. It's the key to a box — a

safe deposit box, where the money is hidden?'

His hands closed about her cheeks. His lips touched hers briefly. Her heart quickened.

'Lady Pen, you're a genius.'

'Lance Patrick, you're too much.'

His arms snaked around her shoulders and they walked back to the sofa together, their bodies touching, the warmth radiating between them, and suddenly Penny felt a sense of great joy, as if they were at the beginning of their relationship, starting again. Nothing was now hidden from one another. His arm remained around her.

'Tell me about the key,' he asked.

'Remember the grubby old bear in the attic? I threw him into the washing machine. You can do that with today's soft toys, but he fell apart. The key must have been hidden in him. Anyway, I cleaned out the bits and pieces, but missed the key, probably because it fell to the bottom and merged into the stainless steel. I found it the next day and slipped it into my jean's pocket. I promptly forgot about it until early this morning. So what's our next move?'

★　★　★

Penny paced back and forward to the front window as she waited for Lance to bring Shelley back to the cottage. When his car finally drew up, she crossed her fingers.

'Here goes. Try to stay calm, act naturally. You're pleased to see Shelley,' she lectured herself as she made her way to the door.

'Shelley,' she cried, 'are you feeling better? I'm so pleased you're home.'

Shelley leaned heavily against Lance, looked up at him and smiled wanly. Acting the ill-fated heroine? A twist of irritation shot through Penny, but she tried to ignore it.

'Thanks for having me. I won't stay more than a few days,' Shelley said in little more than a whisper.

'Well, it's back to work for me,'

Lance said with a grin after settling Shelley on the sofa, covering her with a rug. 'I'm free to return for dinner if anyone's inviting me.'

'He's more than welcome, isn't he, Pen?' Shelley inquired.

'Of course. I'll see you out, Lance.

Penny walked to the door with him, but he didn't leave. He closed it, as if he had, and then crept along the passageway and into the spare room, which he'd set up with the basic necessities for a short stay. He had insisted on being in the house twenty-four hours a day until Shelley left permanently. Experience, he told Penny, indicated that the minute the Anderson woman recovered the key, she'd be out of here.

Penny made a sandwich lunch over which she and Shelley talked about the old days.

'So where's your kid?' Shelley asked finally.

'His gran insists on having him for a few days once a month.'

'Lucky you, eh? All this,' her eyes

ranged around the room, 'and the handsome Mr Patrick, too. I won't play gooseberry for long. By the way, is my car OK?'

'I think so. Lance turned the engine over yesterday.'

'Good.'

She yawned.

'I think I'll go up for a sleep. By the way, you didn't by any chance come across a key when you washed old Bruno, did you? In hospital, I remembered the most astonishing thing. I haven't been able to open my music box in years, not that it's got anything valuable in it, but I was drifting off to sleep one night, and I had this image of stuffing the key into a small hole in teddy's stitching. Don't ask me why. Perhaps we were playing pirates, hiding treasure.'

'Strange you should say that. I did find a key in the machine. I wondered where it came from.'

Shelley jumped to her feet and her voice rose.

'Well, now you know. It's mine. Could I have it back?'

Stay calm, don't push it. Play it the way you rehearsed with Lance.

'I'm not sure what I did with it. It'll come to me. You're not in any hurry for it, are you?'

'I suppose not, but I'd love to know if it's the right key. Come on, Lady Penelope, think. You can't have that many keys floating around. Where do you think you put it? In this room, I'll bet. You spend all your time here.'

Penny nodded.

'Maybe. Didn't you say you wanted to rest?'

Shelley's features tightened, as if she were struggling to curb an impatience.

'I guess I'd better take my wretched pills before I go up.'

She walked across to the sink and started to fill a glass from the tap. Penny felt her heart leap. She held her breath.

'Hey, there's a key here in a glass bowl of junk on the window ledge. This couldn't be it, could it?'

Penny forced herself across to the sink.

'Gosh. So that's where I put it. There you are, Shelley. It's turned up like a . . . I was going to say a bad penny.'

She laughed unnaturally. Shelley hugged her.

'You're a real good friend. Always have been,' she said as she slipped the key into her shirt pocket then added, 'See you later.'

'Shelley, I have some shopping to do. I'll be out for an hour or two. You'll be all right here alone?'

'You go ahead. See you.'

Penny hadn't expected it to happen quite so soon or so easily. So far, so good. She cleaned her teeth, applied light make-up, brushed her hair, and humming gently — a pre-arranged signal to Lance — closed the front door behind her. As she drove towards town, her mobile phone by her side, she took a long breath. Tonight it could be all over. Tomorrow she could bring Jamie home. Tomorrow she could tell Lance she understood his early doubts about her, his dilemma, his commitment to his job.

Tomorrow promised the rainbow's end.

The plan was for her to stay in Lance's room at the Seahorse Inn until she heard from him. She wasn't to go back to the house under any circumstances until he gave the all-clear. She waited, tried to follow a film on television, thumbed through some of his magazines, wondered at his loyalty to his job. She thought of the lonely nights for weeks on end when this was his home, and she loved him for his constancy.

Back at the cottage, Lance heard Shelley Anderson come down the stairs and whispered into his radio connection, 'She's on her way,' and then, at a discreet distance, climbed into his car and followed. Andy was already tailing her and other officers, stationed at strategic points along the highway to

Melbourne, waited for their cue to take up the surveillance.

The knot of anxiety twisted in his stomach. If anything went wrong ... if he couldn't have Penny. He groaned. Think success, mate. His car ate up the miles as the calls kept confirming Shelley's location. The traffic thickened as he neared the city. He speeded up, caught a glimpse of her car as it swung into a carpark, where she got out.

'This one is mine,' he told his fellow-officers as he followed her on foot.

* * *

Penny seized the phone when it rang.

'Yes,' she almost babbled into it.

'It's over, Pen. We arrested Anderson as she opened the safety deposit box. The money's all there. No-one was hurt.'

'What will happen to her?' Penny asked, her voice tinged with sadness.

'She was such a bright girl. She had so much promise.'

'It's time for us to start wondering about what's going to happen to us. Now, you are a very bright girl. I think you know I love you. I want to marry you, sweetheart, make us a family — you, me and the little lad.'

Penny could picture the glint, not of impatience, but of love in his eyes. It had been there before only she'd been too afraid to admit it. Women like her didn't fall in love in a few weeks. But she was no longer the person who had come to Bluff Cottage chasing a dream. She was different because in Lance she'd met reality full on, and it made her feel wonderful, alive.

A few days later, Penny and Jamie were strolling along the Bluff, hand in hand, when Lance appeared.

'Mr Lance! It's Mr Lance, Mummy,' Jamie shouted, running to greet him, seizing his hand. 'Is you goin' to stay at our house? We can play planes.'

Lance picked up the boy, cradled him

in his strong arms.

'If your mummy says yes, I thought we might pack up and go back to my farm. There aren't any pirates, but we've got horses and lambs there. I think you'd like it. Will we ask Mummy?'

Penny watched, her answer already formed on her lips as Jamie pushed himself to his feet and ran to her side.

'Can we live with Mr Lance's amimals? Can we? I'm sick of them silly old pirates.'

Lance was by her side, his arm around her waist, the freshness, the strength of him filling her heart.

'You understand I have to get back to my farm, now my job's done.'

'Not without me and Jamie.'

She smiled up at him.

'You're happy to leave Bluff Cottage behind?'

'I'll put it in storage, along with my childish dreams.'

'But you must never forget them. It's

what makes you such a wonderful little mother.'

'I want to be a wonderful wife, too, Lance. I want to spoil you rotten.'

'A man's going to need more than melting moments and vegetable soup.'

Her mouth curved gently.

'And the man I know will get it.'

He kissed her, gently, whispered her name.

'Why is you kissing my mummy?'

Lance picked Jamie up again.

'Because, little mate, your mummy just said she'll marry me.'

THE END

We do hope that you have enjoyed reading this large print book.

Did you know that all of our titles are available for purchase?

We publish a wide range of high quality large print books including:
Romances, Mysteries, Classics
General Fiction
Non Fiction and Westerns

Special interest titles available in large print are:
The Little Oxford Dictionary
Music Book, Song Book
Hymn Book, Service Book

Also available from us courtesy of Oxford University Press:
Young Readers' Dictionary
(large print edition)
Young Readers' Thesaurus
(large print edition)

For further information or a free brochure, please contact us at:
Ulverscroft Large Print Books Ltd.,
The Green, Bradgate Road, Anstey,
Leicester, LE7 7FU, England.
Tel: (00 44) **0116 236 4325**
Fax: (00 44) **0116 234 0205**

DIVIDED LOYALTIES

Phyllis Demaine

When Heather's fiancé, Adrian, is offered a wonderful job in America their future seems rosy. However, Adrian's brother, Carl, a widower, asks for Heather's help with his small, deaf son. Help which, as a speech therapist, Heather is qualified to give. But things become complicated when Carl goes abroad on business and returns with Gisel, to whom his son takes an instant dislike. This puts Heather in the position of having to choose between the boy's happiness and her own.

THE PERFECT GENTLEMAN

Liz Pedersen

When Laura agrees to help Anthony Christopher to deceive his family she has no idea how far the web of intrigue will extend, or how it will alter her life. His family is as unpleasant as he promised, but Laura drives away from his funeral thinking she has escaped their malicious clutches. However, this is not so. James Christopher is determined to discover what was behind his cousin's precipitate marriage. He despises Laura and hates the fact that he is attracted to her.

THE DOCTOR WAS A DOLL

Claire Vernon

Jackie runs a riding-school and, living happily with her father, feels no desire to get married. When Dr. Simon Hanson comes to the town, Jackie's friends try to matchmake, but he, like Jackie, wishes to remain single and they become good friends. When Jackie's father decides to remarry, she feels she is left all alone, not knowing the happiness that is waiting around the corner.

TO BE WITH YOU

Audrey Weigh

Heather, the proud owner of a small bus line, loves the countryside in her corner of Tasmania. Her life begins to change when two new men move into the area. Colin's charm overcomes her first resistance, while Grant also proves a warmer person than expected. But Colin is jealous when Grant gains special attention. The final test comes with the prospect of living in Hobart. Could Heather bear to leave her home and her business to be with the man she loves?